SPELL STONE

MERRY MAGIC BOOK 3

SHELLEY RUSSELL NOLAN

Join my Newsletter and receive a FREE copy of Arcane Awakenings Books One and Two!

Merry twisted her long hair into a bun at the nape of her neck, grimacing at the unfamiliar colour. Ellen had used a herbal concoction to dye the normally light purple strands a dull brown the night before. It was patchy in places, some of the original colour showing through when she was in sunlight, but Merry wound her black gauzy wrap around her head to help disguise it. From a distance, no one should suspect she was the purple haired witch that was wanted by both the guild and a renegade lord bent on turning himself into a king.

Once her hair was done, she smoothed down the skirt of the long white dress that was the second part of her disguise. She had been given the dress by one of the villagers thankful for her help saving those trapped under the rubble of collapsed buildings. Guilt had thrummed through her at accepting the dress and the other supplies the people of Jeriton had insisted she and her friends should take with them. Not that she begrudged anything the villagers wanted to give Ellen. The healer had worked long days and well into each of the three nights they had been in town to heal the injured, using her newly strengthened heartstone to aid her. Sadie the black cat, her own familiar, had also done her part by entertaining the young patients, smooching up against them, her purr a soothing rumble, as they were treated. They both had more than earned the villagers' gratitude.

It was Merry who didn't deserve their goodwill. She'd been the one to cause the earthquake that had damaged their homes, and trapped and injured many of their people, when she had lost control of her Earth magic at the focal point. If Ellen hadn't intervened, stopping her from causing even more damage, the results would have been disastrous. It was fine for Ellen and Sadie to say it wasn't her fault, blaming the Earth tree instead, but they hadn't been the ones to cause so much pain and suffering to innocent people.

Her inexperience had caused her to create the earthquake when they'd been attacked by Fowler, the renegade Spirit mage working for Lord Andel. In her fear, pain and anger from his mental attack, Merry had let the Earth tree, the physical embodiment of the focal point, channel its power through her and lost the little control she had over what she had wrought. Fowler had been swallowed up by a crack formed in the ground at his feet, but the Earth tree had not been content with his death. The earthquake increased in magnitude, using Merry as its conduit, until the mountains surrounding the focal point rumbled and shook.

Fowler's death had been horrific. He'd been trying to kill Merry and her friends, but to be sealed up in the earth was brutally extreme. It made her stomach churn to think of how he must have suffered, no matter how quick it had been.

The only positive to come out of the nightmare had been her heartstone becoming one of the charms she needed for the transportation spell that would return her home. She couldn't wait to leave Tirana. This world may have provided a safe haven for the witches who had fled persecution in her world hundreds of years ago, but magic and the demands it put on her made it a deadly place to stay. The sooner she could find the next three charms and get out of there, the better.

'Master Roberts is waiting at the Southern gate for us.' Ellen stood beside the door of the small bedroom they had shared last night, the previous two having been spent in a tent while the people of Jeriton worked to make their homes liveable again. Her smile was strained as she looked at the laden pack sitting on Merry's neatly made bed. It was another gift from the people of Jeriton.

Merry was tempted to leave the pack behind, but to do so would insult the generosity of their hosts. With a sigh, she heaved the pack over her shoulder. Then she picked up the wooden staff she had magically carved with a pattern that represented the movement of wind. Not that she'd been aware of what she was doing at the time she'd transformed it from a simple branch to a staff that helped to focus her magic…

She managed a brittle smile for Ellen. 'I'm ready.' She headed for the door, sucking in a deep breath as she made her way to the common room of the inn. They had said their goodbyes to the innkeeper earlier, and she hoped to be able to slip out without notice now.

The common room was empty, and her sigh of relief was heartfelt but short-lived.

As soon as they stepped out of the inn loud clapping began. Shielding her eyes against the glare of the morning sun, Merry avoided the gaze of the villagers as they lined the street. Good natured and heartfelt thanks felt like stones being slung at her, and she winced as each one struck. She wanted to shout at them, tell them the truth, hands gripping the staff so tightly her fingers ached.

Her jaw also hurt as she clenched it against the torrent of words that wanted to spill out.

She was grateful for Ellen at her side, graciously accepting the thanks but not slowing her pace, while Sadie darted ahead. Together they made their way down the short main street, to the gate at the southern end of Jeriton, where three wagons waited. Master Roberts sat in the driver's position in the first one, his hired drivers on the other two. The villagers escorted them to the gate, and it was all Merry could do not to scream as she hurriedly scrambled into the back of the last wagon alongside Ellen and Sadie.

The wagon quickly set off, but Merry kept her head down, not wanting to make eye contact with any of the villagers. She ran her hands along her staff, concentrating on the feel of the smooth wood and the contrast when her fingertips caressed the swirls her magic had carved into it.

'It's okay. We're clear.' A soft touch on her arm accompanied the words and Merry looked up to see Ellen watching her carefully.

The town of Jeriton was receding in the distance, the people still waving from the gate now indistinct figures in dust churned up by the wagons on the dirt road. Behind the town loomed the mountain range that hid the Earth focal point, the mesmerising tree that had used Merry as a conduit.

At the Air focal point, she had been forced to battle a wind golem. At the Earth focal point, she had faced an enraged Spirit mage. Or had her challenge been to resist the lure of the power contained in the Earth tree? If that was the case, she had failed. No, Ellen had said it had been her use of the elemental Earth magic, the earthquake she had created, that had turned the heartstone given to her by the Singers into the charm she needed to make the transportation spell.

Merry had been pleased to receive the heartstone, and to have it attuned to her and her bloodline, after using it to chase Lord Andel out of the Cavern of Heart

Songs. That had been her reward for helping to end the illegal and wanton mining of heartstones. That pleasure had turned to dismay after the events at the Earth tree. She'd been determined to never use the heartstone or her Earth magic again, until she was creating the transportation spell that would help her and Sadie get home.

Then Ellen had persuaded her to use her stone to help the villages, to show it was capable of good as well as bad. It had helped to ease some of her guilt, but Merry was still reluctant to use it again. She was reluctant to use any magic. It came with a price she was not sure she would want to pay if she had a choice. The choice that had been taken from her the moment she accidentally triggered the spell to open the portal that brought her and Sadie to Tirana in the first place. That spell broke after she had used it.

Merry now had to complete a quest to get all five elemental charms before she could make a new transportation spell to return home. Only then would she have a say in her future. She could choose to destroy the portal and forget magic existed or renew the wards at the beginning of each season to keep those who intended harm to Tirana and its inhabitants from using it. Yet even those choices had claws.

The portal on Merry's world existed within *Merry Magic*, the bookshop she inherited from a grandmother she had never known existed until a week ago. Her grandmother had used the portal to escape the guild that was even now after Merry. Soon after she found out she was the sole beneficiary of her grandmother's will, Merry had been approached by *Huntington Inc.*, a company who had caused her to lose her job and her home two weeks earlier, with an offer to buy the bookshop and solve all her problems.

Despite her misgivings about the company representatives and their actions, Merry had been tempted to take the money. Since arriving in Tirana she had learned *Huntington Inc.* were witch hunters determined to complete the eradication of all those with magic that their ancestors began in the Middle Ages. If they gained access to the portal, they would use enslaved witches to open it so they could destroy every witch and mage in Tirana, including Merry's friends.

Even now, the wards were waning. She had to get home before the start of winter, to renew the wards, or to let the guild know where it opened so they could destroy it, trapping her in Tirana forever.

Merry had two of the charms she needed to make her spell. There were Air and Earth. She had to get three more; Fire, Water and Spirit, and then meet up with Ellen's mentor, Debra Mallory, to learn how to make the transportation spell and how to either renew the wards or destroy the portal once she was back in her world.

The next closest focal point was Water. According to their map, it was in Marshland Province, and the fastest way to get to it would be by ship. That was where Master Roberts and his merchant train came in. The goods on the three wagons were destined for Marshland. He was on his way to the harbour at Greystone to load them onto a ship that would deliver them to a harbour in Marshland. Merry, Ellen and Sadie hoped to hitch a ride on that ship.

'Do you really think the captain will agree to take us to Marshland?' Merry asked Ellen. 'What if no one on the ship needs healing?'

That was how they had been bartering for goods and a roof over their heads during their travels so far, except for those nights they'd been stuck in one of the forests that seemed to cover most of Tirana, curled up in a tree hollow or on the flattest and softest piece of ground they could find. Those nights, especially the one where they had been soaking wet after running through the forest in a storm, had not been comfortable. Merry had never been on a sailing ship before but imagined space would be at a premium. They'd need to barter the equivalent value to get passage.

Ellen gave Merry a sheepish look. 'I was hoping the captain would take one look at your dress and jump at the chance to have you as a passenger, especially after we tell them you are stronger than the average Air witch.'

Merry stiffened. 'That's why you asked if anyone had a white dress they could spare.'

Ellen's sheepish look deepened. 'Using wind to speed the ship would be a fantastic barter. All merchants, captains and such, are obsessed with speed. If you promise to get the ship to Marshland faster, I'm sure the captain would eagerly welcome us aboard.'

The captain might like it, but not Merry. Her use of Air magic may not hold as many bad memories as her use of Earth magic had, but still…

'I have no idea how to use wind to speed a ship. For all I know, I'll end up starting a cyclone and smashing us to bits.'

'You'll be fine. Most magic works on instinct. All you need to do is focus on what you want your spell to achieve.' Ellen leaned in and grasped Merry's hand. 'What happened at the Earth tree was the result of extreme circumstances that are unlikely to happen again. No one will be trying to kill us. It will be like when you were helping the Singers get Lord Andel and his men out of the Cavern of Heart Songs. You didn't lose control then, and you won't on the ship.'

The healer is right. Sadie lifted her head, her yellow eyes slitted against the morning sun as she gazed at Merry. *You need to trust in yourself and in your magic. I understand why you might be hesitant, but you did not lose control while at the Air focal point, even though you were under attack. You will not lose control when merely guiding the wind into the sails of a ship.*

Merry gave a nod, wishing it were that simple. With a sigh, she reached into her pack and pulled out the spell box that contained the broken elements of her grandmother's original transportation spell. She had added the two charms she had so far collected to the pile— a feather from a legendary silver falcon, and her heart-stone. Despite coming from a live bird, the feather felt more like metal in her hand. Her heartstone was a blue and purple gem the size of her thumbnail, the colours swirling in constant movement. It was twice the size of the stone Ellen used to augment her magical abilities, and even when it was packed away Merry could feel it, her connection to it a constant presence in her mind. While she always got a sense of power when she held the feather, the heartstone was on a whole other level.

Was it the power of the heartstone that caused her to lose control of her Earth magic or was it because these stones were used to amplify the magic of the one who was holding it?

The stone was a means of connecting you with the power of the Earth tree. You feel its presence more strongly than the feather because you are stronger with Earth magic than you are with Air. All mages tend to have one dominant ability. Your grandmother was strongest with Fire, but like her you have the potential to master all five elements.

Merry narrowed her eyes as she stared at Sadie. Sometimes she forgot the familiar could hear what she was thinking. Many of her thoughts lately had not been meant to be shared.

I spent years advising the most powerful mage Tirana had ever known. Privacy is not a priority when it comes to imparting that wisdom to her granddaughter. Especially when not taking that advice could mean both of us stuck here for the rest of our lives.

Sadie's ears twitched. *As much as I love the land of my birth, there is something to be said for electricity. Winters in Tirana are not kind, and I have become accustomed to indoor heating that does not leave my fur smelling of smoke.*

For the first time in a while Merry gave a genuine smile, imagining Sadie luxuriating in the warm blast of air from a heater. Then her smile faded. The weather had already cooled in the week since she had accidentally transported them both to Tirana. If they didn't get the charms and complete the transportation spell soon, they may not make it back to the portal in time to have the choice of returning. There was no way Merry would risk the lives of her friends and all the other magic users in Tirana. If she could not return to her world, she would have to tell the guild where the portal was so they could destroy it from this side. Then both she and Sadie would be stuck in a world far less technologically advanced than the one she'd been born in.

Indoor heating was just one thing Merry would miss. A proper bathroom was another. She shuddered at the thought of always having to bathe in the draughty sheds that were used as bath houses in Tirana in the middle of winter. It snowed here, whereas the part of Australia she came from barely had a winter at all. What she wouldn't give for a real bathroom, with a steaming hot shower and proper flushing toilets. If she were listing impossible wishes, she'd also ask for a full kitchen equipped with a coffee machine. Her car, too, to make travelling so much easier than walking or being lumped in with piles of goods in the back of a wagon.

Before the guild had destroyed all the portals they could find, when travel between the worlds had been possible, some technology had made its way to Tirana. Lord Andel's manor had a bathroom that would not have looked out of place in any home built in the 1920s back in Australia. But from what her friends had said, only nobles like Andel, rich guild mages, and some of the more prosperous merchant families had been able to afford such luxuries as indoor plumbing. As a witch on the run from the guild, she would have to make do with living rough until she completed the transportation spell and was able to go home.

Merry packed the spell box away and tried to find a more comfortable position against the side of the wooden wagon tray, relieved when the driver called back that they would be taking a break soon. The sun was shining overhead, warming up the day, and her stomach was starting to regret only picking at the breakfast provided by the innkeeper.

Her muscles, after lack of movement for a number of hours, protested as she clambered down. Once she was on the ground, Merry grimaced at the marks she had already garnered on the once pristine white of her dress. White was not a practical colour, but as an Air witch guild law required her to dress in the colour that signi-fied the element. She looked over at Ellen's green dress, still in immaculate condition. But then, the healer would probably manage to keep a white dress just as clean.

Merry surveyed the clearing the three wagons had pulled up in, walking around to stretch her legs as Master Roberts directed his drivers to arrange a place for them to take a meal.

Tirana was beautiful, the lack of technology meaning no pollution marred the pristine sky. The grass underfoot was lush and green, springing back after she walked across it. The clearing was lined with towering trees, their shade a welcome relief from the heat of the sun. While the weather was cool, the sun still had some bite to it.

'Here,' said Ellen, handing out a mug brimming with water.

Merry's tongue did not tingle when she took her first sip, meaning it was not magically imbued to give them extra energy. That was how Ellen had kept them going when they'd had to tramp through forests and run from those seeking to capture them. Lack of food had made them weak, but the spell the Earth witch used on the water kept them on their feet long after they should have collapsed in a heap. They could not rely on magic water too often or it would lose its effectiveness, and their current leg of the journey required no real exertion on their part.

A creek ran along one side of the clearing and Merry wandered over to it, sipping at her mug of water, gazing at the rocky bottom visible through crystal clear water.

Water.

The next elemental focal point she was to visit involved water. She stretched out her senses to see if she could connect with the magic. All she felt was a cool breeze brushing against her, the only sounds the soft burble of the creek and the hum of insects as they skittered over the waterway and through the trees on the other side.

'Merry, the food is ready.'

Merry turned away from the creek and stepped over to where Master Roberts was perched on a cask of ale, munching on a thick slab of meat. Ellen kneeled on a blanket, holding out a much thinner piece of meat sandwiched between two slices of dark brown bread. Merry sank down beside her before taking her first bite. Sadie was perched on the edge of the blanket, nibbling on a small pile of meat that had been shredded and placed in front of her.

In minutes Merry's sandwich was gone and she watched as Ellen handed out the dainty sweet pastries the innkeeper had supplied them with. She also had a jug that contained the chicory favoured coffee commonly brewed in Tirana. It was not as nice cold as it would be hot, and lacked the jolt of coffee back home, but Merry still drank it down.

Then, once the meal was done, they packed up and headed to the wagons. Before they got there the thud of many hoofbeats sounded. Master Roberts, closest to the wagons, took the last few steps at a run, his drivers at his back. He called out for Merry and Ellen to get behind them as they fanned out around the wagons.

A moment later four men on horseback arrived in the clearing. The horses were lathered, sweat mixed with dust from the dirt road dulling their glossy brown coats, the men on their backs slumped over the reins. As one, the men swung down from their mounts and led them to the creek to drink. But even as they took care of their horses, Merry noticed they were also keeping a close eye on Master Roberts and his drivers. One handed the reins of his horse to the man beside him and stepped closer.

'Where are you headed, merchant?' He scanned the laden wagons, and then looked over to where Merry and Ellen stood behind Master Roberts.

'What interest do you have in our destination, good sir?' Master Roberts crossed his arms in front of his chest, chin lifted as he eyed the man. To either side of him the two wagon drivers spread out.

The man lifted his hands. 'I mean no harm. Just a word of warning if Greystone is your intended destination. There's been trouble of late with the guild. It would not be a good time to visit, especially with two young witches in your group.'

Merry and Ellen shared a startled glance.

'What kind of trouble?' Master Roberts asked.

'The kind to be avoided. If I were you, I'd find another town to sell your wares.' With his warning given, he gave a nod to Master Roberts, and then bowed his head in Merry and Ellen's direction, before striding back to his horse.

Master Roberts turned to face Merry and Ellen once the man was out of earshot. 'I'll be continuing on to Greystone. I have to. These goods are already spoken for. But if you choose to heed this warning, I will delay my journey long enough to return you safely to Jeriton.'

Merry shook her head at the same time as Ellen said, 'We thank you for the offer, but like you we need to continue on.'

'Very well. We shall get going then, and hope this trouble is not as dire as that fellow seems to think it.' With that, he led them to the last wagon, waiting until they were settled in the rear before making his way back to the lead wagon.

The four men watering their horses watched on as the wagons pulled away and, like Master Roberts, Merry hoped they had exaggerated the trouble they would find in Greystone. But if the guild was involved, she was afraid getting the captain to allow them passage on the ship to Marshland Province could be the least of their worries.

CHAPTER 2

With the warning they had received, Merry was surprised to find it was not the guild who offered the first obstacle when they arrived at the Greystone town gates later that day. The wooden gates were closed and a group of men wearing black trousers and grey shirts with a white anchor embossed on the front stood across the road before them, with forbidding expressions. Given the warning about the guild causing trouble, Merry and Ellen had put on dark brown woollen cloaks given to them in Jeriton to hide their coloured dresses. Fortunately, the afternoon had turned chill, a wind whipping up for the last leg of their journey, making it reasonable they would be covered up. They hoped.

From the looks of the men barring the way of the lead wagon, this was the local militia.

'Greetings,' said Master Roberts in a booming voice.

'I have urgent business at the harbour. Would you kind sirs be so good as to step aside and allow safe passage?' His tone was even, but there was a hint of forced gaiety to it.

'Greystone is closed to visitors. You'll need to turn around,' called out one of the militia guards as he stepped in front of the line of men, a hand going to the hilt of the sword hanging at his hip. 'By order of the Greystone Council, no outsiders are allowed to enter.'

Master Roberts gave a nervous chuckle. 'Surely that does not apply to merchants such as myself? As you can see, I have goods to deliver, and a captain no doubt impatient to set sail. These goods are due in Marshland the day after tomorrow. If I miss the evening tide, my client will be sorely aggrieved.'

'Your client will be even more aggrieved if your goods are confiscated on account of you declining to obey a direct order.' This was said with a flash of teeth. 'Turn your wagons around, and if you hurry you can get those goods to your client overland within four days.'

'Four days might as well be four years. The client will never buy goods from me again, and will surely blacken my name, if I fail to deliver as promised.'

'That is a problem, indeed.' The militiaman rubbed at his chin; eyes gleaming. 'But it is your problem. Not that of me and my men. Our job is to safeguard the good people of Greystone, and only those that have paid the appropriate council dues can be considered citizens.'

Master Roberts was silent a moment, and his voice

was subdued when he finally spoke. 'If it so happens that I were to pay these dues now, to you, would I then be considered a citizen?'

The greed in the man's eyes gave the answer before he said, 'Why then, as a citizen of Greystone, it would be my honour to open these gates for you, good sir.'

Master Roberts climbed down from the lead wagon and strode over to the man, pulling a pouch from his pocket. Coins clinked as they were handed over. The militiaman pocketed the coins and then ordered his men to open the gates. He stood to one side, watching on with a cruel smile as Master Roberts and the wagons passed him.

'Enjoy your stay,' he called after them, giving a low chuckle.

There was something in the tone, a hint of maliciousness, that made Merry wonder if they and Master Roberts might have been better off to chance the overland route to Marshland after all. But it was too late now. The gate clanged closed behind them and the wagons rattled over the cobbled road that comprised the main street. Like all the places she had been in since arriving in Tirana, Greystone appeared to be set up in a straightforward manner, with the streets in neat lines, though this street sloped downward. In the distance she could see the harbour, the masts of docked ships swaying gently in the swell of the ocean. As they drew closer, she saw the harbour was sheltered on either end by tracts of land, making a horseshoe shape. Buildings were crammed in every available space on the sides of the horseshoe, warehouses from the looks of them, but though there were at least a dozen ships docked there was little activity.

The wind tasted salty, the tang of the sea mixing with a strong fishy scent as Master Roberts led the wagons along the left side of the horseshoe road that ran around the harbour. He pulled up at an empty berth with a number nine made of metal hanging from a signpost. He got out of the wagon and strode to the side of Merry's wagon with a puzzled expression.

'It appears Captain Higgins is late,' he said.

'She's not late,' a gravelly voice said behind them. 'She was just smart enough to get out before the blockade went down.'

Merry twisted around and found a dour faced man with wiry grey hair and a neatly trimmed beard standing on the deck of the ship in berth number eight, arms crossed in front of his chest as he gazed down at them.

'Blockade?' Master Roberts stepped closer to the end of the pier.

The man pointed past his ship, and Master Roberts cursed fervently.

Merry craned her neck and soon discovered what had him so upset. A metal gate was strung across the opening of the harbour that led out to open water. Rusted and covered in barnacles though it was, it still looked sturdy, and from the way it spilled into the water she guessed it went a fair way beneath the surface.

'They pulled up the gate after martial law was declared at midday. No ship is allowed to enter or leave the harbour, until the Greystone militia have completed their investigations into the events of two days ago. Captain Higgins must have got wind of what was happening and sailed at dawn, avoiding being stuck in here like the rest of us. Knowing her, she's found a nice cove to shelter in until this all blows over.'

Master Roberts shook his head. 'Any idea how long this investigation will take? These goods need to be in Marshland in two days.'

The man snorted. 'No hope of that. They're hunting witch folk, and not having an easy time of it. If I were you, I'd forget all about getting your goods delivered and find a safe port to hunker down until the militia have had their fill of terrorising the citizens.'

With a sour expression, Master Roberts banged his fists against the side of the wagon. 'Bloody militia, they knew I'd never get my goods delivered by ship. Not with this blockade of theirs. Looks like we'll be heading over-land after all.' He heaved out a deep sigh. 'I just hope Lady Marsh doesn't blacklist me for not meeting the terms of our agreement.'

'Lady Marsh?' Merry tilted her head.

'Lady Beatrice Marsh. She inherited the title after her father died a year ago and is the ruler of Marshland Province. She ordered all this,' he waved a hand to indicate the three wagons and the carefully wrapped and bundled goods, 'and paid a premium to have it delivered sooner. I will have to return that when I arrive late.'

Merry gave him a sympathetic smile. 'Maybe she'll understand when you explain what happened.'

'Perhaps.' His glum tone suggested he didn't believe it would turn out that way. But with no other choice, he turned the wagons round and they headed back along the main street.

With the words of the sailor in mind, about the militia hunting witch folk, Merry and Ellen kept their cloaks wrapped tightly around their bodies as the wagons approached the gate. A different group of militia guards waited on this side.

'Where do you think you're off to?' one of them called out, stepping forward to bar their way.

'I need to get these goods to Marshland,' said Master Roberts, a hard edge to his words. 'With your blockade preventing me from reaching the ship I had booked to carry them I must take them overland myself.'

The guard gave a harsh laugh. 'The blockade works both ways, merchant. No one enters Greystone and no one leaves.'

Master Roberts gave a splutter. 'What do you mean, no one leaves? I just arrived, not more than an hour ago. Now I wish to leave.'

'See now, I've been on duty here all day, and I don't recall seeing any wagons enter town.'

Master Roberts gaped at him for a moment, and then

shook his head. 'But I paid for entrance. You can check with the outer guards.'

'Did you now? Well then, if that's the case, it appears we have a problem.' The guard straightened, one hand fondling the hilt of his sword.

'I'm glad you—'

'Any caught attempting to bribe those employed in upholding the law of Greystone face imprisonment and seizure of any contraband they may have on their person. So, if you did bribe a guard to let you enter, then that is a very serious offence. Shall I call the outer guard, to determine if such an offence has been committed?'

Master Roberts' face blanched of all colour. 'Ah… no, that will not be necessary.'

With a sly grin, the guard said, 'I suggest you find yourself lodgings, merchant. Once we have rooted out all those who conspired against our fair town, the blockade will be lifted and you will be free to ship your wares.' He let go of his sword hilt and strutted back to where the rest of the militia waited with equally sly grins.

With that, there was nothing for Master Roberts to do but turn his wagons around once again and head back to the centre of town. He pulled over in a side street out of sight of the militia.

'It appears we are stuck here for the foreseeable future,' he said as he approached the wagon where Merry and Ellen waited. 'I have a warehouse near the docks and that's where my drivers and I will be staying while I wait for the blockade to be lifted and for Captain Higgins to return. It isn't comfortable and the amenities are limited, but you are welcome to stay there if you cannot find more suitable accommodation in one of the inns.' He leaned in closer, scanning the street in either direction before adding, 'the gate is not the only way in and out of Greystone, though it is the only one suitable for wagons, unfortunately. Perhaps you can find another way out that will not see you stuck here for the duration of the blockade.' His expression darkened. 'If what we were told is true, and they are hunting magic users, it may not be safe for you here.'

Ellen thanked him for his advice as she stepped down from the wagon and rearranged the cloak around her, tying it securely at the waist. It didn't completely hide her green dress, now that she was standing, but it obscured most of it. Merry did the same, grimacing at seeing the hem of her white dress peeking out from beneath the thick folds of the cloak. Maybe she should dirty it even more than it already was or find somewhere to change into the green dress Ellen had loaned her the day they'd met.

As Sadie lithely jumped down from the wagon and sauntered over to sit in the shadows of a nearby building, Merry and Ellen grabbed their packs and shouldered them.

'Be careful,' said Master Roberts, and then he gave them directions to his warehouse in case they needed it.

They said their thanks and goodbyes and waited

until he had regained his seat on the lead wagon before heading towards the main street to search for a place to stay. They reached the end of the alley and stopped to assess their options.

Greystone was much bigger than any town Merry had been in since arriving in Tirana. There were what appeared to be six inns in the main street, some looking more reputable than others. The disreputable ones were closer to the docks and from where they stood Merry could hear raucous laughter coming from that direction. There were dozens of people about, with the attire of those closer to the harbour a match for the rougher surroundings.

It would be best if I were to wait here, until you secure us lodging. Sadie peeked out from behind Merry's skirt, whiskers twitching as she scanned the busy street. *With all the unwelcome interest in those with magic, it would not do to let the militia or anyone else who may be watching know that you have a companion with you.*

Only those with mage potential were able to hear the mental voice of a familiar, or companion, as Sadie preferred to be called. The black cat had managed to pass herself off as a pet or a stray before, to avoid unwanted attention towards Merry, but that would not be possible in this situation.

Though reluctant to be parted from the familiar, who had acted as her mentor and guide from the moment they arrived in Tirana, Merry knew Sadie was right. *I'll let you know as soon as we find somewhere to stay.*

As she filled Ellen in on what Sadie had said, Merry hoped it wouldn't take long for them to be reunited.

Sadie slunk into the shadows lining the alley while Merry and Ellen entered the busy main street and turned right, starting their search in the better kept section. Shops were interspersed among the inns, selling everything from clothing to food supplies, and even one displayed the healer's leaf. Ellen tried there first, but the door was locked, with no sign of life in the window, and no response when she knocked.

People dressed in a mix of drab greys and browns, with some black and cream mixed in, eyed them as they waited outside the healer's shop, faces grim, bodies tense. Merry saw more than one of them look down and from the dark and suspicious expressions they then shot them she guessed they had seen the green hem of Ellen's dress and the white of hers.

She tugged on Ellen's arm. 'Let's try one of the inns.' If magic users were distrusted, she didn't think they would be able to barter Ellen's healing skills for room and a meal. They did have some of the food given to them by the villagers in Jeriton left and could spend the night in the warehouse with Master Roberts if all else failed. But it would be even better if they could find someone who would be willing to tell them how to get out of town. It would be worth having to sleep in the forest again if they could avoid getting caught up in whatever was going on in Greystone.

They hurried across the road to the first of the inns,

one that had a gleaming sign proclaiming it Greystone's finest. It certainly looked to be well established, the taproom gleaming as bright as the sign and the staff and patrons well-dressed.

But well-dressed did not mean well mannered. The innkeeper took one look at them, with their coloured dresses peeking out from the hems of their cloaks, and chased them outside before Ellen managed to get a word out. Their reception at the next two inns was similar, while in the fourth inn they tried the innkeeper allowed Ellen to say her piece before sneering as he told them his inn didn't accept their kind. Then he spat on the floor at their feet and turned his back on them.

Dejected, they trudged outside and approached the second last inn, one with raucous laughter and the sound of loud conversations spilling out through cracks in the rickety wooden doors. Ellen entered first, and then Merry followed on her heels. She blinked against the sting of smoke and squinted as her eyes adjusted to the dimness inside the crowded taproom.

The volume within lowered for a few seconds when their entry was noticed, and then it got even louder. Merry vainly hoped they weren't the new topic of conversation for those sharing a drink. She wrinkled her nose against the smell of so many people who clearly had an aversion to bathing. Even if the innkeeper was willing to give them a room, Merry didn't think they should stay there or risk asking if anyone knew a way out of town. It was beginning to look as if staying in

Master Roberts' warehouse was going to be their best option.

From what she could see, there were no meals in front of the inn's patrons. This was clearly an establishment meant for serious drinking, and from the stickiness of the floor beneath her boots she figured lots of spilling went on too. Ellen sidestepped the tables clustered through the taproom, making her way to the counter, so Merry followed her. They did not want to be separated by this lot.

At the bar, Ellen tried in vain to get the attention of a man in a cream shirt covered in wet splotches as he stood behind the bar, pouring tankards of a foaming drink and handing them to waitresses in equally wet and stained dresses to hand out to the customers. One of those waitresses scanned Ellen and Merry as she headed back to the bar with an empty tray.

She stopped to stand beside Ellen. 'This is not the place for you, miss. You'd be better off finding Old Clary. If she hasn't gone into hiding like the others.' She leaned in close and whispered something in Ellen's ear, while Merry kept a wary watch on the patrons at the tables closest. Some of them seemed to be taking far too much interest in her and Ellen.

Her gaze skimmed over them, avoiding eye contract as they leered back at her, and then she froze on a familiar face. It was the black-haired driver that had driven a wagon for Master Gin, when they'd left

Pillingston. Travis. She ducked her head and turned away, hoping he had not recognised her or Ellen.

With her hair dyed brown, and in a white dress, albeit one mostly hidden under a cloak, maybe he wouldn't realise who she was, even if he did recognise Ellen. As the waitress finished whispering to Ellen, her friend turned around and pointed back towards the door. Merry wasted no time in skirting through the tables, keeping her body turned away from Travis. She did not take a breath as she wended her way through the smelly mass of patrons and was lightheaded when she finally reached the door and burst out into the fresh air.

Loud laughter chased her down the stairs to the cobbled main street, and she took a deep breath to steady herself, before turning to make sure Ellen was right behind her.

She was. But so was Travis, a wide grin on his face as he bounded down the stairs and came towards her as she hurriedly backed up.

'Imagine my surprise at seeing you here. Thought you were supposed to be learning how to heal in Cambleyn?' His eyes narrowed as he looked her up and down. 'Since when do Earth witches roam around in white dresses?'

Ellen bustled to Merry's side, an easy smile on her face. 'Travis, how nice it is to see a familiar face. What brings you to Greystone? Is Master Gin here? We would love to see him and his lovely wife, to thank them for their assistance.'

Travis never took his eyes off Merry, Ellen's patter of words not seeming to register until she shifted to stand in front of him.

He leaned his head back. 'Never mind what I'm doing here. It's you pair who are going to be in trouble once the militia realise what you are. This place is not welcoming to witches at the moment. And how is it Merry was dressed as an Earth witch last time I saw her, and now she's an Air witch?'

'As I told you before, Merry has only recently begun to discover her abilities. Her use of Earth magic was the first to surface, but it appears she is actually stronger in Air. As I have no aptitude for that element, we have been searching for an appropriate mentor and had heard there was an Air witch in Greystone that may be willing to take her on as an apprentice. We were unaware of the current situation or would have gone elsewhere.'

Merry was impressed with the story Ellen had concocted so quickly. It even sounded plausible. Travis certainly appeared taken aback.

Then his eyes narrowed again. 'That might explain the white dress, but not why she's changed the colour of her hair.'

Merry leaned back when he reached for her head scarf, shooting a glare at him. 'Don't touch me.'

His lips curved into a smirk. 'Happens there are those here who would pay good money to know a witch with odd-coloured hair is in town. From what I discovered in Blackstone, the guild is very interested in you,

Merry.' He rubbed the fingers of his left hand together. 'They paid a pretty penny to learn you were headed to Breezeway, and not Cambleyn like you said.' His smirk changed to a grimace. 'Master Gin fired me when he found out I'd told them where you'd gone. Ruined my reputation while he was at it. But if I were to sell the information of your whereabouts to this new lot, I'd have the coin I need to start fresh.'

He loomed closer. 'Even better, if I can take you straight to them.' He reached for Merry's arm. Before he could touch her, his eyes glazed over and he staggered, a hand going to his head.

Ellen wrapped an arm around his waist and guided him into a narrow street, where she made him sit on the ground with his back propped up against a pole. Then she clasped her heartstone and murmured a quiet spell as his eyes closed over and a loud snore erupted from his mouth.

She straightened up and met Merry's eyes. 'Let's hope anyone who finds him thinks he's just had too much to drink, but we need to be well gone by then. Even better if we could be out of this horrible town.'

Merry heartily agreed and they set off down the street, away from the town centre. She sent out a mental call to Sadie, letting them know where they were, and the little cat was waiting for them by the time they reached the next crossroad. Before they rounded the corner, Merry glanced back at the sleeping Travis.

Putting him to sleep may have solved the immediate

problem, but as soon as he woke he'd be sure to tell whoever it was he thought would pay him for the information that she was in Greystone. From what he'd said, it had to be someone from the guild, and she couldn't rely on it being Gabriel Fairweather. The handsome young mage was the only guild member she would trust not to try to arrest her on sight, though he would no doubt urge her to return with him to the guild tower.

Her cheeks warmed at the memory of standing so close to him while they were hiding from Lord Andel's men that she had felt each breath he took, and the reluctance he'd shown to let go when he'd held her in his arms. Despite them being on opposite sides, she would not be averse to seeing him again. But he had travelled in the opposite direction when leaving the Singers' mountain.

Whoever Travis was going to report her whereabouts to would not be so friendly towards her. They had to find somewhere to hide while they figured out how to get out of Greystone before the guild came looking for them.

CHAPTER 3

'The waitress back at the inn said a woman named Old Clary might take us in,' said Ellen as she led the way through the back streets, stopping every now and then to check street signs. 'She's a retired healer. The shop we saw was hers and is now run by her granddaughter.'

'Did she know why they are hunting witches?' Merry kept her voice low, conscious of hard stares being sent their way by people they passed on the streets. Not that they were the only ones being looked at with suspicion. The people of Greystone seemed to be just as watchful of their neighbours as they were of Merry and Ellen. Still, the sooner they found somewhere to hide out the better. Travis could wake up any minute and run straight to where the guild people were staying to tell them Merry was trapped in town.

'Other than directions, and urging me to get off the

streets as soon as possible, there wasn't time for more questions.' Ellen huffed out a sigh as she stopped at the corner of a crossway, looking in all four directions. 'If I remember right, that should be a saddle maker.' She pointed at the shop on the left corner.

The window display was filled with a variety of unlit candles, some in fancy metal candelabra. No saddles in sight. Merry scanned the shops on the other corners. No saddles were visible in any of their windows either.

'We must have taken a wrong turn,' said Ellen, looking back the way they had come, brow creased. 'Or maybe we missed it.'

Merry didn't remember seeing any saddle places as they'd walked, but then she had been more focused on the people.

I believe we are lost. The black cat had kept pace with them, slinking along in the shadows cast by the rapidly dark-ening afternoon to avoid unwanted attention. Even knowing she was there, Merry found it hard to pick her out.

While she agreed with Sadie's words, she didn't repeat them for Ellen's sake. The young healer looked distressed enough as it was. 'Maybe if we backtrack, we can start again.' Not that she liked the idea of returning to where they had left Travis sleeping in the alley. But maybe a few streets would be sufficient for Ellen to find her way.

Ellen shook her head. 'We don't have time for that. It's going to be dark soon. If this healer doesn't give us a place to stay, or know someone who might, we will have to keep going. I do not want to be roaming the streets once night falls.'

Merry didn't like the sound of that either. 'If we can't find her, we'd be better off heading to Master Roberts' warehouse. At least then we would have somewhere to hide if the guild come looking for us.'

Ellen straightened up and strode into the path of a middle-aged couple heading their way. 'Excuse me, would you happen to know where we might find Mistress Clary?'

The woman gave a start, hand coming up to cover her mouth, eyes wide, while the man put his arm around her and glared at Ellen. 'Get away from us, girl. We don't consort with the likes of you,' he said, casting a glance at the others on the street before pulling the woman around Ellen and then scurrying off.

Others in the street moved to the other side of the road, gazes averted, clearly not wanting Ellen to approach them next. Her shoulders slumped, and she turned back to Merry. 'You're right. We should head to the warehouse.'

Merry gave a nod and then looked down each of the crossroads, trying to determine which one would lead them closer to the harbour. They'd taken so many twists and turns to get where they were, she wasn't sure what direction it would be, and it was clear no one would help them.

She could no longer hear the noise from the disreputable inn where they had stumbled across Travis, and with shadows darkening the street it was getting harder to see. But she thought she could hear the cry of gulls and gestured for Ellen to follow her as she walked in the direction of the sounds.

The street they were in took a turn, narrowing as it split into a series of alleys. The buildings on either side were smaller, constructed from timber rather than stone, their walls jutting against each other, the window displays a jumble of goods. Clearly, this was a less affluent area, but she was heartened by the noise from the gulls getting louder, and the sea salt tang rising in the air. They had to be heading in the right direction.

Merry picked up the pace, turning into the next alley, grinning when the buildings started to increase in size. This must be the beginning of the warehouse section. Down the end of the alley, she could see the mast of a ship gently swaying in the ebb and flow of the harbour and the fishy scent she'd noticed before was back.

'We're nearly there,' she said as she glanced over her shoulder to Ellen.

Look out.

At Sadie's warning Merry spun to face the alley again, and then scrambled to a stop as five men poured out of a doorway to block the narrow alley. Ellen clutched her arm and Merry turned around, only to discover another four men standing behind them.

They were trapped between the two groups, and an angry mutter rose from the men.

Merry sucked in a breath, hands gripping her staff as

she prepared to create a wall of wind to ward off an attack. It warmed beneath her fingers, and she could also feel a hum from the heartstone tucked away in her bag. Energy from the stone flooded through her as she turned sideways, backing up to the building behind her, so she could keep an eye on both groups and no one else would be able to sneak up on them, with Ellen close beside her.

Dark expressions covered the men's faces as they closed in.

'Who are you? What do you want?' Despite her intention to sound cool and unafraid, Merry's voice shook. She didn't want to use her magic to hurt anyone. What if her Earth magic lashed out at them and she lost control? The rickety timber buildings in this area would not fare well if she accidentally set off an earthquake, and even with her heartstone Ellen would not be able to put all nine men to sleep.

Merry wished she'd thought to get Ellen to teach her that spell while they had been travelling to Greystone, instead of stressing over the damage she had caused back in Jeriton. Rendering their foes unconscious would be far preferable to using her Air magic to force them back and risk her Earth magic slipping off its leash. Even now, the hum was intensifying, the thrum vibrating through her body, seeking an outlet.

She sucked in a deep breath, pushing down the urge to lash out with her Earth magic and make the ground shake beneath the feet of the men.

'Look at you two, thinking we're too stupid to notice you're both bloody well witches.' The man in the lead spat on the ground, the gross globule landing perilously close to Merry's boots. 'You act as if you're better than us, just because you have magic and we don't,' he said as he waved a hand at the men at his back. 'It's your stinking magic that has us locked up in our own bloody town. How are we supposed to make a living, feed our families, when we can't bloody well take our boats out to catch fish to sell at market? We're going to starve, and it's you bloody witches' fault. You should be the ones in lockdown. Not us.'

From the smell of his breath, the reddened eyes and the sway of his unwashed body, not being able to catch fish to sell hadn't stopped him from drinking copious amounts of alcohol. Merry pushed that thought aside when he leaned in close, looking as if he was going to spit directly in her face this time. No way was she going to stand there for that.

Wind whipped around her, ruffling her headscarf and blowing the edge of the cloak covering her white dress aside.

Merry's eyes widened. That gust of wind had not come from her, but the goose bumps sweeping over her body said it was magical in nature. She gasped as a second group of people, twice in number of the ones accosting her and Ellen, stepped into the alley. They were all dressed in nondescript clothing, no coloured shirts or dresses among them, but at least one of them had to be an Air witch.

'Get out of here, Darren,' an old woman at the front of the newcomers said, her face a mask of determination. 'Stop harassing these girls or I'll set a pox on your backside that will have you itching and unable to sit down for a month.'

The man who had spat towards Merry blanched, hands moving to cover his rear. Then he recovered his bluster. 'You can't tell me what to do. I'll call the militia, and tell them you threatened me. I've got witnesses.'

'Witnesses?' The old woman snorted. 'Witless as you, the lot of them. I'll pox them as well, if they breathe a word of this. Don't think I won't.' She turned her glare onto each of the men in turn. 'Now get out of here, before I decide to do it anyway.'

The nine men slunk off down the alley, though the one called Darren sent a dark stare at both Merry and the old woman as he went. Threat of an itching pox or not, Merry was sure he would run straight to the militia and report them.

'Clary,' said one of the people who accompanied the old woman, 'you can't keep threatening to pox everyone who doesn't agree with you.'

The old woman glared at the woman who had spoken. 'It's the least they deserve, after believing the lies those militia are spreading about us. I've healed the good people of Greystone for sixty years, and this is the thanks

I get. Forced to hide in my own town, forbidden from practising magic, all because some idiot decided it would be a good time to start a witch hunt. 'Tis not right.'

So, this was Old Clary, the healer the waitress had told Ellen to find. Not that she appeared to be in a position to help them if she was in hiding, as her words suggested. But then, she had run off Darren and his friends.

Old Clary waved a hand at Ellen and Merry. 'Don't know how you girls wound up in this mess, with the town gates locked and guarded, but you're here now so we'll have to make the best of it. Come along now, before Darren and those other idiots remember what a backbone is for.'

She turned around and set off, not stopping to check if Merry and Ellen were following along. But then, what choice did they have. It was either go with her or try to find Master Roberts' warehouse and hope they didn't encounter any more townspeople with a grudge against witches.

They set off down the street after Clary as the people with her crowded around them. A cool wind was still whipping through the streets, and Merry could see some of their escort were murmuring things under their breath. Spells, she was sure, from the goose bumps still washing over her. She had no idea what the spells were meant to do, other than someone having wind at the ready, but no one accosted them or even glanced their way as they hurried through the rapidly darkening streets.

Merry remembered when she had been hiding in the tunnels with Gabriel, hoping the guards for Lord Andel wouldn't find them. Gabriel had said she'd created a spell, with the litany she'd been saying in her head. Maybe one of the people around them was doing the same thing. Either way, she was glad no one paid them any attention as they reached yet another alley and were ushered through a door to narrow steps that led below ground.

One of their escort gave a startled gasp as Sadie shot between his feet and darted down the steps ahead of him. He was quickly shushed by Clary, who gave Merry and Ellen a considering look as they followed the familiar.

Light flared ahead of them. Not bright, but enough that Merry didn't stumble on the uneven stone steps. She reached the bottom, Ellen at her side, and entered an equally narrow hallway that led to a stout wooden door. A large man, holding a staff three times as thick as Merry's, stood in front of the door. He was so tall his head nearly brushed the ceiling of the hallway as he stepped aside and opened the door.

Despite his intimidating size, the broad smile he gave was welcoming as Merry, Sadie and Ellen were ushered through into yet another hallway. This one was wider, with numerous doors on either side of it. Most of them were closed, but Clary led them to one that was open on the far left, gesturing them to enter ahead of her. Inside, a blonde woman wearing a flowing purple dress sat at a large square table. She looked to be around Merry's mother's age, and her eyebrows rose as first Merry and then Ellen entered the room.

The woman gasped when Sadie jumped up on the table in front of her, and then she eyed Clary with a wry grin. 'Well, this was not what I was expecting when Bethany sent word that you'd found trouble. Not that I didn't expect you to find trouble. Just not a guild mage.' Her eyes narrowed as she looked from Ellen to Merry and then to Sadie. 'Whose familiar are you, then?'

I prefer the term companion, as you should well remember, Donna Syphera.

Sadie's mental voice was tart.

The woman, Donna, gave a start. 'Sadie?' Hope blossomed on her face. 'Is Meredith with you?'

It was Merry's turn to give a start. This woman had known her grandmother, and she had to be a mage, not a witch, if she could hear Sadie's mental voice. Only a strong mage would be able to converse with a familiar not her own.

I am afraid Meredith is no longer with us. I am here with her granddaughter, Merry. Her first visit to Tirana is not turning out as I imagined when I arranged to bring her here. Being stuck in a town while witch hunts are taking place was not part of the plan.

'Wait. What?' Merry shook her head, not sure if she had heard Sadie right. 'You arranged this?'

The black cat's body stilled for a long moment, and then she twisted her head to gaze at Merry, her yellow eyes unblinking. *I did not plan to have us stuck here with a broken spell box. Or get us involved in ridiculous witch hunts. The idea was to gently introduce you to your heritage. Not to have us traipsing all over Tirana to get the charms needed to make a new transportation spell, while being chased by guild enforcers or imprisoned by lordlings who would be king.*

Merry gaped at Sadie as she thought back to when the spell box had suddenly appeared on the table in her grandmother's kitchen, and how the familiar had tripped her as she'd gone to investigate it. Merry had cut her palm on the brass lock of the spell box, her blood triggering the transportation spell. She'd thought it had been an accident. But it had been Sadie's intention to bring her to Tirana all along.

Sadie's left ear twitched as she continued to gaze at Merry. *You should never have been raised ignorant of your heritage. I was merely seeking to remedy that deficiency.* Her tone was matter of fact, unrepentant.

'By transporting me to another world against my will. You had no right.'

I had no way to get your permission. Not then. I needed you in Tirana before the familial bond would connect. But if you hadn't let go of the spell box it would never have been broken. We would have been able to return to your world once I was able to communicate with you.

'Oh no, you do not get to blame me for this.' Merry glared at the little cat. 'We're stuck here because of you.'

Sadie narrowed her eyes and glared back at her. *Better to be stuck here, and know the truth of who you are, than to live with no idea of your potential. Your grandmother should have been the one to instruct you in the ways of magic. Your father's stubbornness robbed her of that chance. Her promise to him, to not have any contact with you, made the last years of her life miserable. To know you were so close but to be unable to reach out to you was a nightmare for her; a nightmare I watched unfold year after year. Meredith wanted nothing more than to lavish you with all her love and share her knowledge of magic with you. Instead she was forced to watch you grow up from a distance, forbidden to talk to you or to even let you know she existed. You have no idea what that was like for her, how each passing year crumbled the hope your father would relent. In honour of her memory, I decided that when you were finally made aware of your relationship to her, I would do everything in my power to ensure you fully understood all you had missed out on.*

Merry reeled at the blast of words coming from Sadie, a torrent of emotional pain coming with it and a grief so overwhelming it choked her. She swallowed heavily and then cleared her throat, voice raspy as she said, 'I'm sorry for what happened to her, but that was not my doing. Yet I'm the one being punished because of your decision. I've been ripped from my home, and I have no idea if I will ever be able to return. How is that supposed to honour her memory?'

Before Sadie could respond the woman named Donna held up a hand. 'How you both came to be here and who should be blamed is a discussion for another time. We have more important things to worry about. The militia are rounding up every magic user they can find. We need to free the ones they've already caught and get out of Greystone before they come after the rest of us.'

'You know a way out of town?' Ellen moved to stand beside Merry.

Donna nodded. 'There is a smuggler's tunnel that leads to a cove a short distance away. We have a ship waiting there to take us to Marshland Province. But we are not leaving without the rest of our people.' She looked behind Merry. 'Did you find where they are being held?'

Clary pushed past Merry. 'The militia have them all locked up in the gaol. They've tripled the guard and may increase them again if Darren and his fellows tattle about how we rescued this pair,' she said, jerking her head to indicate Merry and Ellen. 'But it couldn't be helped.'

'Are the militia working for Lord Andel?' Merry asked, forcing down her anger at Sadie and the situation the black cat had landed them both in to focus on their current problem.

Donna frowned. 'Why would you think that? Andelmine is a long way from here.'

Merry told her about the magic users going missing in Andelmine and being forced to swear oaths to obey Lord Andel. 'He won't be able to make the oaths binding, without more heartstones, but there are some mages and witches who are working for him willingly.'

Donna's frown deepened. 'This is troubling news indeed, but I've seen no sign of any of Andel's men. Though I doubt he is the only lord to have an eye for taking a throne. No, we've had trouble with enforcers instead.'

'Enforcers?' Merry and Ellen shared a glance.

'Aye. Stirring up trouble. As if we didn't have enough of our own. Though it does make me wonder who the instigator of our current woes might be.'

'What do you mean?'

'There was an accident.' She shook her head, sorrow darkening her expression. 'Innocent people died, and from the circumstances it appeared magic was involved. While the militia was looking for someone to blame, our brethren caught the brunt of the backlash. People who have known us all our lives turned their backs on us, sure we'd used magic against their neighbours. We were working to uncover the truth, to find out who really caused the accident, when the enforcers showed up and started throwing their weight around. Next thing we know the militia had declared martial law, put Greystone in lockdown, and were rounding up any magic users they could find. Those of us that could escape fled here, but others were caught. Now it is up to us to see they aren't punished for the doings of others. But mark my word, once I find out who dared besmirch the good name of these people, there will be a reckoning.'

From the hard tone and the militant glint in her pale blue eyes, Merry didn't doubt her sincerity.

Donna's face was tense as she looked to Merry. 'Getting our people out from under the noses of so many guards will not be easy. The cells themselves are warded against magic, so our brethren will not be able to assist us until they are freed. You are a Meadows witch. If you have half the potential of your grandmother, you would be a valuable member of the rescue party.' She was silent for a moment, and then she said. 'I will help you get to Marshland so you can find your next charm. In return, I want your help to rescue our people.'

Merry grimaced at the offer. But she had no choice. 'Fine. I'll help you.'

The lines on Donna's face eased and relief shone in her eyes. 'Thank you.' She smoothed down her purple dress, a dress that marked her as a witch and not a mage.

Merry waved a hand at Donna's dress. 'If you can hear the mental voice of a familiar not bound to you, why aren't you a guild mage?'

'Like your grandmother, I did not agree with the direction Ophelia Fairweather was headed. But unlike her, I was not at Ralinin when the enforcers came to force obedience. By the time I learned what had happened, it was too late to help them. Meredith and many of my friends had been captured and taken to the tower, imprisoned, while I hid, donning the dress of a witch to hide my identity. Am I proud of that, no, but when opportunity arose I made amends by helping her and those who had managed to resist swearing an oath escape from the guild tower. For that I have been hunted by those I once considered friends, always running, always hiding. But that will bear us in good stead now, as I never enter any town until I am sure I have a way to leave undetected if needed.' She gave a bitter smile. 'Turns out being born to a smuggling family has its advantages.'

Donna appeared confident, but would those advantages be enough?

Merry hoped she would not regret getting caught up in the rescue attempt. She just had to hope nothing went wrong.

CHAPTER 4

As Donna worked with Clary and the others on the plan to free their friends, Merry stood to one side of the door and leaned against the wall, Ellen at her side, wondering what role she was going to be asked to play, hoping it would not involve Earth magic.

We need to talk.

Merry stiffened, hands clenching into fists as Sadie crossed the table and stood in front of her. The black cat's eyes were wide and unblinking.

No, we don't. Anger flared anew at the way the familiar had manipulated her.

A soft sigh sounded as Sadie lowered her head, tail gently swishing from side to side. *I cannot lie and say I wish I could undo what I did. Especially now I know witch hunters are sniffing around the portal. But I do regret not telling you the truth when we first arrived in Tirana.*

Having said her piece, Sadie stood and moved across the table to stand in front of Donna once more.

As apologies went, it wasn't great, but now it was Merry's turn to sigh.

However it had come about, she was stuck in Tirana for now and had to do whatever she could to make sure she got home. The sooner the better. It was clear the whole country was on the brink of a major upheaval. The mage guild was losing control, and lords like Andel were plotting to overrun them and seeking to undermine them from within. She had to get home before the situation went from unstable to explosive.

This was not her world. Even though events kept putting her in a position where she was confronted by the warring sides, it was not her problem. But being angry at Sadie for bringing her here didn't stop her worrying about the repercussions the coming conflict was going to have for the friends she had made since her arrival.

Ellen had done everything she could to help Merry since they'd met, even agreeing to accompany her on the quest to get the five charms she needed for the transportation spell. She'd left her injured mentor to fend for herself in the haunted Spirit enclave at Ralinin to do so. There had been no way to contact Debra, to see how she fared with her broken ankle. No way of knowing if she had been recaptured by the guild, caught up in the upheaval by Lord Andel or one of the other scheming lords, or was slowly making her way to the guild tower so she would be in place when Merry finally made it there with the elemental charms. Both Ellen and Debra were risking their lives to help her. When it was time for her to go home, she would be leaving them in a more precarious world.

Then there was Gabriel Fairweather. He was a guild mage. Whatever the lords were planning would affect him directly. The fact he was Ophelia Fairweather's nephew had already made him a target of Lord Andel's machinations. If Andel was successful in destroying the guild and having himself named as king, Gabriel could find himself in a dark predicament. She'd only known him a short time, and he'd been attempting to arrest her for most of it, but he was a good person. Honourable. To think of him being forced to swear an oath to obey Andel and having to wield his magic against his will was distressing.

Merry was also worried about the rebels who had been captured by Andel's militia. Britta may have been determined to force Merry to join her group to fight back, but she didn't deserve to be locked up in that stinking dungeon until Andel could find more heart-stones and another Spirit mage to force her and the other imprisoned witches to swear the oath to obey him. She didn't see him letting any of them go because he had lost access to the mine and his mage was dead... dead because of what Merry had done.

Merry pushed all those thoughts aside, reminding herself this was not her world. Not her problem. It was enough that she had agreed to renew the wards on the portal in her grandmother's bookshop to stop the witch hunters gaining access to Tirana. Although if she decided not to stay in Belwich and run *Merry Magic*, she would have to destroy the portal completely. But that was a decision she would face in the future. For now, she had to help this group of magic users free their friends so she could resume her journey to the Water focal point. One step closer to her goal to go home and then decide what she wanted to do with her life, and whether she wanted magic to remain a part of it.

Donna approached her and pointed at the staff Merry still gripped in one hand. 'Sadie tells me you are strong in both Earth and Air. Mage potential. We could use both those strengths to minimise the risk to all of us. Most of the witches here have only limited mastery of their elements. None of them has heartstones like you and your friend.'

Merry grimaced. She had been so focused on her own thoughts that she hadn't caught the mental conversation between the cat and Donna. She didn't like the idea of Sadie spilling all her secrets to this woman, even if she had been a good friend of her grandmother's.

'I will go in first, and neutralise as many of the guards as I can,' said Donna. 'Then the others will sweep in. Healers, like Ellen, will focus on sending those they can reach to sleep. We don't want the townspeople more upset with us than they already are, so we need to minimise any injuries to the guards. I'll want you to focus on Air, creating a wall of wind the guards cannot penetrate to protect the healers.'

'I can do that.' Merry was relieved she wasn't asking her to use Earth magic. Wind she was more confident she wouldn't lose control of.

'Excellent. It is time to go.' Donna rounded up the dozen witches who were to attempt the rescue, ordering Clary to lead the rest of them to the cove via the smuggler's tunnel.

Sadie regarded Merry with unblinking eyes. *Perhaps it would be best if I were to travel to the cove with this group. I can make sure the area is safe before you join us, and I would only get in the way during the rescue.*

Given Merry's conflicted feelings about the little familiar and what she had done, some distance between them would be good. Still, if something were to happen to stop them meeting up again, would it be worth it? Could she continue on her journey to get the charms she needed and return to Belwich without Sadie?

With a sigh, Merry gave a nod, knowing that no matter how strained their relationship might become, she would do her best to be reunited with the black cat. Sadie said nothing more as she joined Clary and the others, and her group soon disappeared down the hallway.

Merry went in the opposite direction with the rescue team. She stepped into the large cellar after Donna opened the door and gaped at four men and two woman who were clustered at the base of the narrow stairs leading to ground level. They were all dressed in mundane clothing, and Merry might have thought them to be more of Donna's people if not for a familiar face in their midst.

Travis wore a smug expression as her gaze met his.

'Who are you? How did you find this place?' Donna strode past Merry and confronted the group. 'You're not from Greystone.'

No, they were from the guild. They may have been wearing plain clothing, but she could see the glint of silver from the sword pendant hung around the neck of the young man standing beside Travis.

Enforcers.

Merry's stomach roiled as the former wagon driver pointed at her. 'That's her,' he said, 'the witch the guild has been looking for.'

As one, the enforcers shifted their stares to Merry. The young man with the visible sword pendant stepped forward, hazel eyes narrowed. 'You are the granddaughter of Meredith Meadows?'

Donna stepped in front of Merry, head high. 'Her bloodline is none of your concern. You do not belong here, enforcer.'

He glared at her. 'The guild has full authority over those with magic, and she is from the bloodline of a traitor. We have every right to take her into custody.' One of the enforcers at his back muttered words too low to hear, and he softened his stance. 'But that is not why we have come.'

A bitter twist to his mouth, he said, 'We need your help.'

Donna gave a low chuckle. 'I bet that hurt. You guild lot aren't so good at begging.' She crossed her arms in front of her chest. 'What makes you think I would lift a finger to help you?'

'I have people ready to inform the guards where you are hiding. Turn us away and you will have nowhere left to hide. Help us get out of Greystone, and I will ensure the guild is made aware of the aid you rendered.' His square jaw clenched; lips puckered as if he tasted something sour in his words.

'You're enforcers. Can't you force your way out of town?' Donna's tone was threaded with amusement, giving no sign she was intimidated by his threat. 'It's what you do, after all.'

His gaze darkened. 'It appears renegade mages are working with the Greystone militia. Our previous attempt to leave ended in failure. They are also preventing us from contacting the guild to request reinforcements. Mage Fairweather must be informed about these traitors, and their attempt to undermine the guild stopped. But we cannot do that if we are stuck in this stinking town. Those that help us get free will be rewarded by the guild. Get in our way...'

From the way she tensed, Merry was sure Donna knew retribution would be swift. They were facing six enforcers now, with no idea how many more waited in the streets above. Donna wouldn't want to risk them telling the guards where they were hiding, not when she was determined to rescue the rest of her people.

'Fine,' said Donna, chin raised. 'We will get you out of Greystone. But not until we have freed those of us the militia have already imprisoned. Do you have a problem with that?'

If he had a problem, he was wise enough not to say it.

Travis was not so wise. 'Hang on, I thought you just wanted Merry.' He looked from the enforcer to Merry. 'You said I would be paid if I led you to her.'

The enforcer grimaced. 'You will be well paid, once I am able to contact the guild and arrange for someone from the tower to meet us with funds.'

'That will take days, even if you do make it out of Greystone. I need money now.' His eyes went to slits as he surveyed those lined up behind Merry and Donna, and that smug smirk returned. 'You're all witches. The town council has a bounty on your heads.'

Before he could say anything more, Ellen brushed past Merry and placed a hand on his arm. Travis' eyes rolled back in his head and the square jawed enforcer lurched forward and caught him, lowering him to the ground.

The enforcer's eyes glinted with amusement as he turned to Ellen. 'That was quick thinking.'

Ellen blushed and gave a shrug. 'It was nothing. Any healer could have done it.' Then she moved back to stand beside Merry.

The enforcer's gaze lingered on her for a moment, and then he turned to Donna. 'We will assist you in freeing your friends.'

There were unhappy mutters from the other enforcers at his words, but Donna quickly accepted his offer to help. In a few terse sentences, she explained the plan she had come up with. Then she led her increased team out of the building and into the street. Night had fallen while they'd been in the underground haven, and Merry stared at the shadows as they neared the next alley, waiting for guards to appear. There were no streetlights in this section of town, though she could see the flickers of fires and lamplight in the windows of some of the buildings they passed.

They hit a crossroad and Donna put up a hand to halt their progress just before it. She closed her eyes, her lips moving in a silent murmur for a moment. Goose bumps swept over Merry until Donna opened her eyes and beckoned them on once more. The mage must have used her magic to sense if the way was clear.

Merry had avoided using her magic since helping to fix the damage she had caused with her earthquake in Jeriton, but she didn't like having to rely on Donna's ability to guide them without being detected by the Greystone militia or townsfolk like the drunken Darren. They were a large group and, as much as they tried to be quiet, noise was inevitable. She cast out her senses, and in her mind's eye she could see the glimmer of people in the buildings around them. The streets remained empty until she sent her consciousness further ahead. In the distance was a large group of people, and in their midst were flashes of colour that indicated magic users. This must be the gaol.

They still had a fair way to travel to reach the gaol, and the element of surprise could be lost if any of the people in the buildings they passed looked out a window and raised an alarm. Merry began a litany in her head.

Do not see us. Do not hear us. Do not see us. Do not hear us.

She focused as much of her attention as she could on her litany, hoping Gabriel was right when he said it was possible to create a spell without having to speak the actual words. Unlike when other people were using magic, there were no goose bumps to indicate if hers was working, but Donna did glance back at her, a shrewd look in her eyes.

The mage led them through the streets faster after that, only to pull up with an audible gasp when two militia stepped out of the doorway of a building right in front of her.

Pressure built in Merry's head when the two men looked their way, her mental litany practically a shout.

One of the men peered directly at Merry for a moment, eyes narrowed. Then he shook his head before turning and walking in the opposite direction, his companion close at his heels, the pair debating which tavern they should go to. They soon disappeared down a cross street and Merry exhaled her breath in a rush, the pressure in her head easing.

'Can you keep that up when we reach the gaol?' Donna asked in a low whisper.

'I think so.'

'Good. I want you to enter the gaol with me.'

'What? That wasn't the plan.' Was the woman crazy?

'I came up with that plan before I knew you could create a cloak of invisibility for two dozen people. If you can do that, you are far more valuable on the incursion team. You can get me inside the building with no one the wiser. We won't have to fight our way inside. Once we're in, the others will distract the guards, giving us the time we need to get our people out of there.'

She didn't wait to see if Merry agreed, turning to the young enforcer who had bargained with her. 'Getting my people free is the priority. I am trusting you to safeguard this lot, while Merry and I see to the others.'

The enforcer sent a considering look Merry's way before he turned back to Donna and gave a grim nod. 'I give you my word, we will do our best to protect your witches.'

With his agreement, Donna set off again. They continued another two blocks, Merry keeping her litany going, and then stopped in the rear courtyard of a building that spanned the corner opposite the gaol. As the rest of their group huddled in the dark, waiting until it was time to create their distraction, Donna gestured for Merry to follow her.

Back straight, showing no sign she doubted Merry's ability to shield them from the eyes and ears of the militia guarding the front of the gaol, Donna strode across the road.

There were two militiamen standing on either side of the closed front door, while two more stood at the edges of the building. An awareness in the back of Merry's head warned her there were more guards on the roof of the stone building, and the pressure built as they turned their gaze towards the street where she and Donna were.

Do not see us. Do not hear us.

Merry had to tighten her focus as the pressure continued to build, no longer trying to hide the enforcers and the witches waiting in the shadows. It took everything she had to keep herself and Donna hidden. Despite the cool of the night, sweat coated her skin and a headache began pulsing behind her eyes.

'Just a little farther,' whispered Donna.

A few more steps and they were at the front door. It remained closed, the militiamen guarding it staring down the street, hands on the hilts of their sheathed swords, stances vigilant as they waited for trouble. Trouble was slipping between them.

As Donna reached for the door handle, Merry stretched her senses to include it, so the guards wouldn't wonder why it opened with no one there.

The interior was well lit, lamps hanging from the ceiling and shining down on a number of desks. These were currently occupied by the militia, some of them with their heads cocked towards the door. Merry faltered, the litany in her head stopping for a split second. She hadn't calculated on guards being inside.

Stupid. She'd known there were non-magical people inside the gaol from when she had scanned ahead.

She quickly strengthened her litany, but two of the men were already lurching to their feet, alarm on their faces.

Donna stretched out a hand, and the alarm turned to horror as the men batted at their heads, a high-pitched keen erupting from the lips of one of them. The other dropped to the ground, cramming himself under his desk. The rest of the men in the room jumped to their feet, running towards the stricken men, as Donna calmly strode through their midst, headed for a barred door on the other side of the room.

They were halfway there when a man wearing a purple robe stepped into their path. 'Really, Donna? A nightmare spell? How very childish.'

'But very effective, wouldn't you say?' Donna's voice was calm, even as screams came from the militia who had sought to aid their comrades.

A nightmare spell. Merry shuddered to think what it was the militia were seeing that had them screaming. But it had to be better than having their brains scrambled as Mage Fowler had done to her. Even the memory of it made her head hurt. Though that could also be because she was still maintaining the invisibility spell. It appeared not to work on the Spirit mage facing Donna.

'Merry, get the keys from that man there,' said Donna, pointing to where a man was curled up in the corner of the room with his head tucked under his arms, body shuddering. 'I'll take care of this rubbish.' She stiffened her shoulders and strode closer to the other mage, hands stretching towards him. For his part, he wore a gleeful smirk as he imitated her stance.

The goose bumps that swept over Merry were so intense her entire body shuddered as the two mages worked their magic against one another. She pushed her discomfort down and ran to the cowering man in the corner to get the keys. Her fingers fumbled, but she eventually got them off the loop on his belt and then ran towards the barred door. She could hear sounds of fighting in the street outside, the promised diversion. They had to work fast, before the militia got reinforcements.

There were numerous keys on the ring, and it took Merry a moment to find the right one. She hurried through, entering a cellblock that was much cleaner though no less crowded than Lord Andel's dungeon. Men and woman in a multitude of coloured clothes stood up as she ran to the first cell and went through the keys on the ring. There were numbers etched on the keys that matched numbers on a sign above each cell door, so she soon had all the captives released.

Once the last witch was freed, Merry ushered them back to the door into the front room.

The guards were still cowering on the ground from whatever nightmares Donna had sent them, while the two Spirit mages stood on opposite sides of the room, grimaces on their faces as they threw invisible attacks at each other.

At no point during her time unlocking the cells had the goose bumps let up. But now it began to come in waves. Both mages were tiring, and from the slump of Donna's shoulders she was finding it difficult to battle her opponent while at the same time keeping the guards down.

Merry pointed the freed witches to the front door. 'Get out of here. I'll help Donna.' Even as she said the words, Merry prepared a gust of wind and threw it at the renegade mage.

Alarm filled his eyes and his arms flailed as he was pushed backward. Donna surged forward and placed a hand on his head. He dropped to the ground, and the goose bumps besetting Merry lessened as Donna turned to her with a weary smile.

'Thank you for the timely intervention.' She then hurried to the closest of the guards and touched him on the arm. He soon slumped down unconscious. Once she had done this to the others, she moved to the front door.

'Hurry up, they need us outside.'

It was chaos when they stepped out of the gaol and hurried down the stairs. Militia guards were lined across the street, keeping the freed witches from reaching the others. The witches were fighting back, but they did not have the strength to go up against the guards.

Donna waved a hand, and some of the guards cried out, but others gave no sign whatever spell she had cast affected them. 'It's no use,' she said with a groan as she rubbed at her temples. 'I'm exhausted. If I push myself any further I'll burn out. You'll need to get us through,' she said to Merry.

Her head had stopped throbbing as soon as she had dropped her invisibility spell, but as Merry focused on calling up a huge gust of wind the ache started up again. She pushed through the growing pain, sweeping the middle section of guards to either side to create a gap she and the others could run through.

On the other side of the street, the enforcers stood in a protective line in front of the rest of their troops, hands clenching as they used their telekinetic ability to toss militia this way and that. Merry grimaced, remembering how it had felt when Kassandra had used telekinesis on her. It was as if a giant hand had grasped her and held her immobile.

The ache in her head intensified, and she stumbled as she ran, but Donna grabbed her arm and steadied her. 'Keep going, we're nearly there.'

Merry worked to speed up. They were falling behind the other witches. She did not want to be left behind and captured by the militia. She was maintaining her wind to push them back, but its force was lessening. If they didn't get clear soon, they would never make it.

Fear lent her strength and she pushed past the last of the combatants, and then reunited with the other witches.

'Now!' Donna roared.

As one, the enforcers pointed at the ground between them and the militia, then they clenched their fists as they raised their hands and the road lifted up in response. Alarmed shouts came as the startled militia fell back from the gaping crack, and in the ensuing confusion the witches and the enforcers ran for their lives.

CHAPTER 5

*A*fter two minor skirmishes with the militia, Donna led the way to the entrance to the smuggler's tunnel, hidden inside an old stone building that jutted up against the town wall. There were numerous sighs of relief as the weary witches and enforcers hurried into the dark depths. Merry gripped her staff, using it to light the way, though even that small piece of magic caused the ache in her head to throb even more. She was thankful when the witches lit lanterns and she could let her light go. Not that the throbbing in her head went away. Her limbs were also weary, making it feel as if she had wrestled those militiamen with her body and not her magic wind.

Somehow, she ended up trudging through the dank tunnel alongside the leader of the enforcers. He kept shooting glances her way, though every time she turned to look at him he averted his gaze. A prickle went over her at his actions. The prickle turned to outright unease when she looked over her shoulder to find the rest of the enforcers at her back. But if they had ill intentions, there was nothing they could do about it now, stuck in the tunnel as they were.

Donna had assured them the militia would not be able to find the hidden entrance to the tunnel, or even be able to open it if they did. The magic that secured it was keyed to her bloodline and all her family members were with her. One of the freed witches had been her son, while her daughter, Bethany, had led the first group to safety.

After they had walked for what felt like hours, Donna called a halt. Merry pushed through the witches in front of her, glaring at the enforcers when they made to follow, and slumped against the tunnel wall beside Ellen.

'How are you holding up?' Ellen asked. 'If you need it, I have some heartleaf you can chew.'

Merry gave her a weary smile. 'I should be fine. I just wish this headache would go away.'

'Here, let me.' Ellen reached out a hand and placed it on Merry's forehead. 'I felt useless during the battle. My magic is not made for combat situations. But headaches I can help with.'

Warmth flooded Merry's head, spreading down her neck and to all her limbs, taking her pain with it. This was the first time Ellen had used her healing magic on

Merry since she had her heartstone rejuvenated by the Mistress of Songs and the effects were much stronger.

'Being able to heal people is far better than using magic to fight them,' Merry said. 'Trust me, what you can do with your magic makes a huge difference.'

Ellen gave a pleased smile. 'My heartstone is what makes the difference. But thank you.'

Though her muscles were no longer sore, and her head had stopped aching, Merry was still tired. She stifled a wince when Donna announced the break was over and it was time for them to get moving again. A yawn broke free as she got to her feet and they continued on through the winding tunnel. It was wide enough for four people to walk side by side, no doubt for the ease of the smugglers who had once used it to get their contraband in and out of Greystone.

Merry walked alongside Ellen, glaring at the enforcers when they pushed through the witches to get behind her once more. That lot was going to cause trouble. The lead enforcer was practically stepping on her heels, though now she was walking beside Ellen he was splitting his gaze between the two of them. His light brown hair was drenched in sweat from his exertions, and not just the trudge through the tunnel. He and the others had been instrumental in their escape, ripping up the road on more than one occasion to stop the militia from following them. Still, she would not rest comfortably until they parted ways.

Ellen stumbled, giving out a low gasp as she toppled

sideways. Before Merry could reach out to help her friend, the lead enforcer was on the other side of Ellen and steadied her with one hand.

'Careful,' he said. 'We can't afford for our best healer to be injured.'

Ellen gave a breathless laugh as he released her arm, 'Thank you, Adrian.'

He gave a slight bow and remained at Ellen's side as they continued on. Though Merry was glad he had stopped her friend from falling, she kept a close watch on him, not trusting his motives. There were no more stumbles, but Adrian and his enforcers remained close through three more rest stops.

Merry was so tired she thought she was hallucinating when they finally reached the end of the tunnel and Donna slid aside a large wooden door. The pale light of dawn shining through the opening was as beautiful as a mirage. They'd walked all night, and still had farther to go.

'We can rest once we're on *Hellcat*,' Donna told Merry as she wearily lined up behind the witches waiting to step through the door. 'Sadie informs me that Captain Higgins has longboats on the beach ready to ferry us to the ship. The people we sent through with our gear last night are already onboard.'

Merry stumbled as she stepped out of the tunnel, but no enforcer rushed forward to steady her. She gave a wry shrug as she used her staff to keep her upright on the rocky ground. A stand of bushes obscured the opening and she hurried around them with Ellen at her side, pleased when the enforcers got caught at the exit. The rocks soon gave way to sandy grass beneath her feet and a squat dune loomed ahead of her. Her breath came hard and fast as she clambered to the top of the sand dune and got her first look at the cove and the sailing ship waiting for them. A ship with a fitting name.

Hellcat.

Once they were on board she would be reunited with Sadie, and she still wasn't sure how she felt about that in light of what the familiar had done. It appeared Sadie was also in two minds, as she had telepathically imparted her information to Donna and not Merry.

The first group of witches to exit the tunnel were clambering aboard two long boats pulled up at the water's edge, and from the size of them it would take at least two trips to ferry them all. Merry scanned behind her, to where Adrian and the other enforcers were coming around the bushes before she set off down the other side of the sand dune. She hoped she would be on one of the longboats before they caught up with her again.

But she was halfway down the beach when the two longboats set off.

Damn.

She stopped just short of getting her feet wet, Ellen at her side, as the longboats were rowed out to *Hellcat* and began the laborious task of getting the passengers transferred.

Her misgivings were confirmed when the enforcers grouped near her and Ellen, their gazes making the skin between her shoulder-blades twitch. They were planning something.

She was tired, the aches having returned to her muscles thanks to walking all night, but she gripped her staff and prepared to fight as Adrian stepped closer, determination in his gaze as he raised a hand.

Alarmed shouts came from the witches making their way down the sand dune, Donna among them, and their pace picked up, though many of them stumbled rather than ran thanks to having walked all night. The source of their alarm was soon apparent when a swarm of men in uniform appeared on top of the sand dune, showing no sign of slowing as they barrelled after the fleeing witches.

The militia from Greystone.

They'd found them.

Adrian cursed, flicking a black stare Merry's way, before he clenched his fist. One of the militia guards at the front of the pack went reeling, even as the rest of the enforcers joined in and tossed other members of the militia aside. As more militia swarmed over the dune, Merry knew the enforcers would not be able to stop them all.

She was more exhausted than she could ever remember being, but she had to do something. She sucked in a deep breath and gripped her staff with both hands, holding it horizontally in front of her as she sought the last of her reserves to call on the wind.

It was hard at first, the element sluggish to respond, but she mentally commanded it to obey and soon a strong breeze answered. It whipped through the air and battered the militia not already stopped by the enforcers, giving Donna and the beleaguered witches time to reach the rest of them. Donna immediately turned around and stood beside Merry, many witches gathering to either side of them, while those with magic that would not help them in this fight huddled behind them on the water's edge.

They couldn't flee. They had to stand their ground long enough for the longboats to return to gather up the rest of them.

Merry never let her wind rest, using it to whip up the sand between her and the militia and fling it at them. There were cries as the men rubbed at their faces, hands raised to shield them from the sand. To the left of Merry, the enforcers reached out with their telekinesis and rendered some of the militia immobile. But there were more militia than there were enforcers.

Goose bumps ripped over Merry's skin as Donna muttered something too low to hear, and soon some of the men fell screaming to the ground, terror-stricken expressions on their faces as they battered at invisible nightmares. Then the Spirit mage Donna had fought back at the gaol appeared on top of the sand dune, and with a wave of his hand the magical attack from Donna was cut off. The militia surged forward, anger distorting their features.

Merry continued to throw sand at them, whipping it into a whirlwind that lashed at their exposed skin, though she winced at the welts she could see rising from it. She didn't want to hurt anyone. She just wanted to get away. But what they were doing was not working.

The heartstone in her bag hummed with life, its tantalising call wrapping around her, begging to be used. After what had happened last time, Merry was wary about unleashing it, but maybe here on the sand she couldn't cause too much damage.

As another mage, this one dressed in an orange robe, appeared beside the Spirit mage, Merry knew she had no choice. The Fire mage had a small ball of flame sitting between his hands, the fireball growing bigger as he worked on it. Merry did not want to see what would happen when it got big enough for whatever he planned to do with it. She had to use her Earth magic.

It would take too long for her to dive into her bag to retrieve the heartstone from the spell box, but Ellen was able to use hers by placing a hand on her bodice, the heartstone necklace tucked away on the other side.

Merry shifted position, grounding herself in the shifting sands as she placed one hand on her shoulder bag, feeling the hard edges of the spell box, seeking her connection with the heartstone. Her awareness of the stone strengthened, and she pulled on its power as she visualised all the sand on the beach in front of her drawing together to build a massive sand dune, one that would block the militia and the renegade mages from coming any closer. A soft scraping sound filled the air as billions of tiny grains of sand obeyed her mental command, rushing through the air to create a dune twice as large as the one she had envisioned.

Water pooled around Merry's ankles, soaking into her boots and wetting the hem of her dress, while a buzz settled into her body. Salt danced in her tastebuds and she realised she was tasting the sea water. With the militia fenced off on the other side of her dune, she risked a backwards glance and saw that she had pulled the sand from behind her as well, meaning the waterline was now higher. She could see the longboats, drawing closer, almost within reach of the witches who were now standing in the shallows.

'Look out!' Donna's panicked shout had Merry's head snapping around, gasping in horror at the sight of a fireball flying through the air towards her.

She acted on instinct, reaching down to pull at the water milling around her ankles, forming it into a spout and throwing it into the sky to meet the fireball at the peak of its arc. Steam flared as the sea water extinguished the flame and then fell to the ground in a salty deluge that drenched Merry and those standing near her.

Merry wiped the heated sea water from her face as she readied herself for another attack.

Behind her she heard Donna urging the others to get

onto the longboats, but she did not turn around. She was ready when two smaller fireballs arced over the sand dune, one from either end. She split her consciousness, drawing water up in two spouts and blasting the fireballs from the sky.

She staggered and would have fallen if not for Adrian lunging forward and grabbing her arm in a hard grip. She was soaked, from sweat as well as sea water, and her limbs felt as boneless as a jellyfish. She fought to remain alert, eyes narrowed as she waited for what would come over the sand dune next.

The grip on her arm shifted, grabbing her around the waist and lifting her high.

'Hey!' Merry wriggled in the enforcer's grasp.

'I'm trying to save your life,' he said, his voice a rasp.

She pushed wet hair off her face and saw that he was carrying her to the closest longboat, and she stopped resisting. He dumped her over the side, and she landed in the bottom with a thud that forced the air from her lungs. She scrambled to her feet and frowned at him when he jumped over the side with ease and settled in the seat beside her as the longboat began to move towards *Hellcat*.

'There was no need to be so rough,' she said as she glared at him.

He glared right back. 'Would you rather I left you on the beach to face that?' He pointed behind her and she twisted around to see the militia had reached the top of her magically formed sand dune, swords drawn as they ran down the other side and approached the waterline. The renegade mages followed more slowly, trudging down the dune, weariness in the slump of their shoulders. From the looks of the one in the orange robe, Merry didn't need to worry about him tossing any more fireballs at her for a while.

But the militia showed no signs of giving up. Swords held high, faces tight with anger and determination, they reached the waterline and ran into the shallows.

Merry readied herself to use whatever she could to keep them from reaching the longboats, but when she tried to call on her magic all she got was a wave of dizziness. She reeled sideways, only to be steadied yet again by Adrian.

'We'll handle this,' he said, raising his free hand and pointing at one of the militia guards who was almost close enough to touch the stern of their boat. The man froze mid-step, and then toppled sideways when the enforcer abruptly released him. He gave a gurgled yell when he crashed beneath a wave. Around him, more members of the militia were toppling over as the longboats pulled away.

Soon the boats drew alongside *Hellcat* and the weary witches and enforcers began the laborious task of climbing aboard via a number of rope ladders flung over the side.

Still dizzy, Merry wasn't ready to attempt the climb when it was her longboat's turn to be unloaded. She was exhausted and miserable, salt and sand chafing her skin with each movement she made. All she wanted to do was get her wet clothes off, have a long hot shower and then crawl into a soft bed. She doubted she'd be lucky enough to get even one of those things on *Hellcat*.

She let the witches go first, and soon it was only her and the enforcer who'd carried her onboard left on the longboat. Merry waved for Adrian to go ahead of her, but he merely folded his arms in front of his chest.

'I don't intend on taking a swim to retrieve you from the bottom of the ocean,' he said. 'I've already swallowed enough sea water to last me a lifetime.' The rasp to his voice was testament of his assertion.

Merry shook her head. 'So?'

'You can go first, and try not to fall off.'

Merry frowned at him as she got to her feet, gripping the side of the longboat as she made her way to the end of the rope ladder. Every part of her ached, but she ignored her pain as she gripped the first rung. The rope was stiff, wet and crusted with salt, much like Merry herself, but she began her climb. She was not going to let the arrogant jerk behind her see how her arms trembled, and there was no way she was going to fall.

The pain radiated in waves over her body, and the climb seemed to take forever, but Merry finally reached the railing and was helped over the side by Ellen. A rush of warmth swept through her and she stepped away from the railing feeling somewhat rejuvenated. Ellen's magic might be stronger now, but only true rest would heal her body completely.

Her head felt two sizes two big as she scanned the deck, gaze skipping over witches huddled against the railing or slumped against piles of rope and rigging. At the base of wooden steps that led to the wheelhouse, Donna was talking to a woman in a striking black and grey jacket, with big silver buttons, a split black skirt revealing grey leggings beneath it, and knee-high leather boots.

As Adrian clambered over the railing, Merry and Ellen walked over to Donna and what had to be Captain Higgins.

'Is that everyone?' the captain asked a man in a grey and black striped tunic and grey trousers.

'Aye, captain. That's the last load.'

'Good. Get us out of here before that lot gear up for a second round.' She indicated towards the beach to where the militia had left the water and were clustered in a group around the two mages. 'I don't fancy having to dodge fireballs while the '*Cat* makes for clear water. Though you seem to be handy at dousing those things.' Now she looked to Merry. 'I also hear you're good with wind and can get us to Marshland in half the time.'

Ellen gave a shrug when Merry looked her way. 'You are wearing a white dress. It wasn't as though I could hide the fact you can do Air magic.'

Donna laid a hand on the captain's arm. 'Merry has done enough for tonight. My people will make sure the wind blows in your favour as we journey to Marshland.'

'Marshland?' Adrian barrelled over to them. 'We

need to go to the guild tower. The guild must be informed about these renegades.' He waved a hand in the direction of the beach. Then his gaze fell on Merry. 'There are other matters that need to be brought to their attention urgently. I demand you head for Crystal Harbour.'

'That's in the opposite direction to Marshland,' said Donna, arms crossed in front of her chest and a forbidding look in her eyes. 'Besides, we've already hired Captain Higgins and her ship. You want to go to the guild, find your own ship.'

'Mage Syphera, you are a traitor to the guild. You are under arrest and will be taken to the tower to be punished as you deserve.'

'You're not doing your cause any good by insulting my paying guests,' said Captain Higgins in a droll tone. 'Our course is set.'

He turned his glare on her. 'You would be ill-advised to go against the guild, captain.'

'The guild has no right to interfere in a transaction fairly made between two parties. That is the agreement your illustrious leader drew up when she first took control of the guild. I am carrying out the transaction as ordered, with Mistress Syphera. Taking you on board, at considerable threat to my ship and crew, was an act of goodwill. In a second such act, I will drop you and your fellow enforcers at the next cove. You will be able to travel overland to the guild tower much faster from there than you would from Marshland. Now, if you will excuse me, I have a ship to tend to.' After ordering a crewman to show her paying guests to their rooms, the captain strode off.

As Donna ushered Merry and Ellen to the steps that led below decks, Merry caught the dark look Adrian sent their way. He was not happy about the circumstances and she was sure he had plans that did not align with those of Donna or Merry.

But that was a problem for later. Merry was only too happy to be shown into a tiny cabin. She was less happy to find Sadie perched on a desk bolted to the wall between two sets of narrow double bunks. Two of the beds were occupied, and Donna indicated for Merry and Ellen to take the other two.

'Rest. I'll come get you after we reach the next cove. The less that enforcer sees you the better.'

'He's not too happy with you either,' said Merry, failing at her attempt to stifle a yawn.

'I've been on the run from his kind for the last twenty years. I have more than a few tricks up my sleeve. Rest well.' She left the room, closing the door behind her.

Ellen clambered onto the top bunk, fully clothed, and Merry did the same on the bottom bunk. She was still wet and bedraggled but too tired to care. She could worry about that after she'd had some sleep. She closed her eyes, conscious of the movement of the ship as it left the sheltered cove and made for open water, hoping the movement Dent wouldn't worsen and make her sick.

Merry, you were right. I should never have brought you to Tirana the way I did. I should have made an attempt to communicate with you back in your world, allowed you to make up your own mind whether you wanted to learn more about your heritage. I took that choice away from you and landed us both in a difficult situation., For that, I am very sorry. I hope you can forgive me. Meredith is gone. The life I once lived gone with her. You are all I have left. I don't want to lose you as well.

Merry gave a soft sigh. *I'm sorry too, for yelling at you, and you aren't going to lose me. I'm angry, yes, but I'll get over it. Eventually. Just be straight with me, from now on. Okay?*

Of course, Merry. A wash of relief came with Sadie's words, and Merry felt the black cat land on the bunk near her feet. The familiar curled into a ball, head resting on Merry's leg, her low purr wrapping around the confines of the tiny cabin.

As she let sleep take her, Merry hoped that when she woke all her problems were as easy to solve.

CHAPTER 6

Merry woke with a start, heart thudding in her chest as she opened her eyes and scanned the dark cabin. She shifted, feeling the warmth and heaviness that was Sadie still sleeping nestled against her calf. She could hear the soft breathing of her roommates, Ellen above her and the two witches in the bunks on the other side of the cabin. None of them stirred, so that couldn't have been what woke her.

A soft creak came from beyond the closed cabin door, and Merry strained her ears at a soft swishing sound, one that suggested the movement of cloth against cloth. Was someone outside the cabin or was it the movement of the ship's sails and the creaking of timber that had woken her?

The creak came again and Merry squinted as a dull light edged around the side of the wooden door. Someone had opened it, and the sound of cloth rubbing against cloth came again. Then she heard an indrawn breath that did not come from her roommates. Someone was about to enter the cabin, and from the stealth of the entry they were not there with good reason.

She flung aside her blankets, eliciting a startled meow from Sadie, and bolted out of her bunk as the intruder strode inside.

A force gripped her around the middle, stilling her forward momentum and squeezing the air out of her lungs. Lanterns flared to life in the hallway, allowing her to see the smug smirk on Adrian's face. Two of his enforcers were at his back and more crowded in the hall behind them. Frightened yells came from the witches who shared the cabin with Merry. From their garbled curses, she knew they had been similarly immobilised.

'Merry, I can't move,' called Ellen.

Neither can I. A snarl accompanied Sadie's words. *When I get free, I am going to rip these enforcers to shreds.*

Merry fought with her magic, calling wind and throwing it at Adrian. He merely grimaced, squinting his eyes, and tightened his fist. That tightness spread to the hold around Merry and she could no longer breathe, no longer concentrate to use her magic. Her wind stuttered and died. With her resistance gone, Adrian backed up, his telekinetic ability pulling her along with him. He stepped into the hallway, while Merry struggled to gasp in air against the punishing and yet invisible grip he had on her. There had to be a way to fight him. But how?

She was inexorably pulled towards the door of the cabin, brushing past the two enforcers who were keeping Ellen, Sadie, and the two witches immobilised.

'What do you think you are doing?' Donna's shout came from somewhere in the hallway outside the cabin.

'This witch is wanted by the guild. I have full authority to arrest her and any who interfere.' Adrian's voice was calm, clearly not worn out by the force he was using to subdue Merry and drag her along with him like a recalcitrant dog on a lead.

'You are not taking her. You need to get off this ship now, before I lose my temper.' Donna's voice was just as calm as the enforcer's, but it had a deadly edge to it. 'We gave you safe passage. We have kept our part of the bargain. Do not test our wrath by breaking yours.'

'She is an enemy of the guild.'

'She is a young witch finding her way. If that makes her an enemy, then every witch on this ship is an enemy. We will not let you take her.'

Goose bumps swept over Merry, and not just due to the magic she could feel building in the hallway beyond her cabin. The cold determination in Donna's voice chilled, making her fear just how far the Spirit mage was prepared to go. As much as she didn't like Adrian and the other enforcers, she did not want Donna doing something to them that would get her in even more trouble with the guild.

There had to be a way for her to break his hold. Enforcer magic was akin to telekinesis, while that of witches and mages was elemental in nature. Throwing wind at him hadn't achieved anything, and she didn't think using her Earth magic would work while they were at sea. As her lungs cried out for air, she pushed through the pain and cast out her senses.

To her surprise, she realised they were anchored in a cove that was similar to the one in which they had boarded *Hellcat*. She could sense the land beneath the hull of the ship as it rose beyond the water to where it met scraggly grass and then turned into a rocky outcrop. Life pulsed beyond the cove, the spark of both magical and non-magical people as well as animals. None of that helped her stop Donna from engaging in a fight with the enforcers that would put them on an even worse standing with the guild.

She was dizzy, oxygen deprivation making her head spin and her vision blur. She couldn't breathe. She was going to suffocate. Panic clawed at her as she reached out with her senses one more time, this time seeking the spark that was Adrian as she imagined him feeling what she felt, as if she was drowning.

A roar came from behind her and then a stream of water flew through the air and hit the enforcer, covering his face.

He lifted a hand to shield his mouth and the force around her middle eased enough for her to suck in a breath.

As quickly as it had come, the water fell to the

ground, startled curses erupting from the enforcers and witches gathered in the hallway.

Then there was a loud thud, and the force around Merry vanished completely.

She dropped to the floor, now slick with sea water. Had she called it? Her head was still spinning, but she remembered thinking how she wanted the enforcer to experience what she was feeling. She turned her head and could see him on his knees in the corridor, a hand going to his head. Adrian was drenched, but there was still fire in his eyes as he glared at her.

Before he could do anything to her, Ellen stepped past Merry and laid a hand on his forehead. He slumped to the floor, expression slack.

As Merry gathered herself to her feet, Ellen put the rest of the enforcers to sleep one by one.

'Well done,' said Donna. 'Now to get them off this ship before they wake up and cause even more trouble.'

All hope of getting back to sleep lost, Merry headed to the top deck and watched on as witches bundled the sleeping enforcers into one of the longboats. Ellen clambered on board as well. 'I'll make sure they stay asleep,' she said, settling on a bench where she could easily reach them all, though she sat closest to the slumbering Adrian, a conflicted expression on her face.

Ellen was joined by the sailors, dawn approaching as the longboat was lowered over the side. Merry remained on deck, Sadie at her side, as the longboat was rowed to the beach. The sailors deposited the enforcers on the sand, out of reach of the tide, and then rowed quickly back to *Hellcat*.

Ellen and the others were back onboard, the longboat being raised, when Merry spotted the enforcers groggily getting to their feet. Even at this distance she could see the anger in Adrian's posture, and she half expected him to reach out with his magic to grab hold of her again.

Nothing happened and they soon set sail for Marshland, leaving the enforcers behind. But she was sure she hadn't seen the last of them. That was a problem for another time. She headed below decks and was grateful to discover the ship had rudimentary bathroom facilities. It was by no means an easy feat, but she managed to wash off the worst of the salt and sand crusted to her body, though her hair was a lost cause at the moment. Some of the dye Ellen had used to colour her hair brown had been washed away in her drenching in salt water, the purple shining through, but as she was on a ship, far from those who wished her ill, that wasn't as concerning as getting into a clean dress.

She felt almost normal when she ventured above decks in the green dress Ellen had loaned her when she first arrived in Tirana and was handed a warm bowl of thick porridge sweetened with honey. There was even a mug of chicory flavoured coffee, though whoever had brewed this batch had made it much stronger than what she'd been served at the inns they'd stayed at. She gulped down her porridge and then leaned against the rail to stare at the water as she sipped her drink.

'The guild will not stop looking for you, especially once Ophelia is informed you can now access three of the five magic elements,' said Donna as she joined her, a steaming mug of coffee in her hands as well. 'She will suspect you would be able to master all five, like your grandmother, and consider you far more of a threat than mages like me who only have mastery of one. She'll not have forgotten the acclaim and honour your grandmother was accorded because of her abilities. The sooner you can return to your world, the better it will be for you, but I would be remiss in not trying to recruit you. Someone with your potential would go a long way towards getting the guild to reduce their stranglehold on magic users. And if what you told me about Lord Andel is true, that he wishes to reinstate the monarchy and is using enslaved magic users to help his cause, then those of us without guild favour need your help even more.'

Merry made to speak, to say this was not her fight, but Donna raised a hand and cut her off.

'I'm not asking you to decide now. You have three charms still to collect before you can make the spell to take you home and, like Debra Mallory, I will help you in any way I can if that is your wish. But as you collect those charms, and see more of Tirana, I want you to consider the good you could do here, the persecution you could help prevent if you were to join with us. I do not condone what Sadie did, bringing you here unaware of what you would face, but this world is part of your heritage. Your grandmother was imprisoned for decades because she believed witches and mages deserved the right to wield their magic as they see fit, within mutually agreed guidelines that ensured no harm to themselves or others. The guild seeks to take that choice away from us, while lords like Andel wish to use us for their own gain. Think on what part you could play, that is all I ask.'

Donna walked away, leaving Merry to resume her survey of the glistening ocean. The coffee tasted extra bitter on her next sip as she contemplated what the Spirit mage wanted from her. She had landed in enough trouble as it was, just trying to get to each of the elemental focal points. To contemplate taking on the guild, or Lord Andel, was crazy. She had no idea what she was doing, her use of magic one of instinct powered by desperation.

Heritage or not, she did not belong here, and she couldn't imagine this was what her grandmother had wanted, by leaving her the bookshop. Surely if she had been thinking that Merry could be a part of the resistance, she would have tried to prepare her, not leave her ignorant of magic or that Tirana existed.

Merry spent most of the day at the railing, watching the distant coastline drift by, or staring at the waves as they rolled away from the bow of the ship. At night she retreated to her cabin, allowing the rocking of the boat to soothe her to sleep. The next morning she once again took her place at the railing to eat her breakfast and contemplate what might await her in Marshland Province.

Ellen and Sadie joined her when lunch was served, hard bread and a spicy soup served in the same mug her coffee had been in. The bread softened well enough in the soup, and the meal served to heat her up from the inside and helped ward off the chill wind that began to blow. When it was clear Merry was not in the mood to talk her friends drifted away and she once again resumed her silent contemplation of the water.

As she stared at the cresting waves, Merry narrowed her eyes. There was a sheen on the water, almost like an oil spill, but glowing with a blue green light. At first the sheen appeared in small patches, but they grew in size during the afternoon.

Nausea swirled in Merry's stomach the longer she stared at the sheen, and a sense of misgiving enveloped her. Something wasn't right.

She called Ellen over. 'Can you see it, the sheen?'

Ellen stared down at the water. 'You mean the way the afternoon sun makes it reflect like tiny sunbeams?'

'No. The blue green glow. It's creepy, sickening.' A hint of rot arrived on the wind and Merry covered her mouth and nose to ward it off.

'I can't see anything,' said Ellen.

'But you can smell it, right?'

Ellen's brow creased. 'All I can smell is the sea.' She

grimaced. 'And far too many people who have not bathed recently.'

Was that it?

No. The stench was not that of sweat or dirt. It definitely put Merry in mind of a rotting heap. She cast out her senses towards the nearest patch of shining water and gagged at the rising stench. She hurriedly pulled her senses back, doubled over, fighting the urge to empty her stomach over the railing.

'Maybe you're seasick. I can help with that.' Ellen placed a cool hand on Merry's head and warmth soon flooded her body. But when Ellen removed her hand, and Merry straightened up, she could still smell the rotting stench coming from the oily patches of water. Worse, there were more patches of it than there had been before.

As she looked towards the coast, Merry spotted dead fish floating on the surface. Birds wheeled above them, but none of them gave the fish or the boat a second look, seeming bent on flying in the other direction, away from the coast.

They were headed to where the water was clear, Merry was sure.

More birds followed, a mass exodus that soon had many onboard *Hellcat* exclaiming in surprise. As they passed, one flock of birds fell from the sky. Some landed in the water. Others hit the masts and sails and careered off to land in a broken mass of feathers on the deck of the ship.

A sailor bent over to poke at one of the birds.

'Don't touch it.' Merry pushed away from the railing and ran towards the downed bird. 'Don't touch any of them.'

At least a dozen birds were scattered over the deck. The sailors and the witches crowded around the bodies. Merry reached the closest bird and reeled back as a waft of rot came from it. The bird shone with the same blue green light as the water. She covered her mouth, working not to retch.

Donna appeared at her side and clasped her elbow. 'What do you see?'

'It's rotten. Can't you smell it?'

Donna shook her head.

'But you can see the shine on it, right?' Merry asked.

'All I see is a dead bird.' Donna scanned the deck. 'Lots of dead birds.'

Merry explained what she could see and smell, both on the birds and the patches of water. 'It's as if they're diseased.'

Donna drew back. 'Some kind of poison?'

Ellen leaned closer, stretching out a hand and holding it just above the bird. Merry tensed, not wanting her friend to touch it. But the healer soon withdrew her hand and turned to face them.

'It's as if the organs all shut down, but there is no indication as to why. The bird was healthy.' She looked at the rest of the carcasses on the deck. 'I think you're right,' she said to Donna. 'It is some kind of poison, but not a natural one.'

'A magical poison? Is that even possible?' Merry frowned.

'I'm afraid so,' said Donna. 'Generations ago, some mages used vile spells to poison the enemies of the king. But the guild outlawed their use once they took power. It is concerning, to think a mage out there has broken the law and unleashed this on Tirana.' She called the captain over and urged the need to avoid direct contact with the dead birds. The sailors dealt with the carcasses, using tools to pick them up.

To Merry's dismay, they threw them overboard, adding to the miasma of death in the water around the ship. All the witches lined the railings, Donna ordering them to look for the shine, but other than Merry, there were only two others who could see it. Even then they could only see it once she pointed it out.

These two were Water witches, but not strong. Still, it was enough to determine that the water itself was poisoned. As they drew nearer to the coast, the shine grew so thick and bright, the stench of it so strong, Merry had to go below decks to get away from it. Yet the smell seemed to seep through the timber. She was glad when the cry came that they were soon due to land at the main harbour for Marshland Province.

That relief died out after she and Ellen gathered their things and hurried back on deck to find the harbour filled with the rotting carcasses of fish and birds. The stench of the dead animals was bad enough now that even Ellen and the others could smell it. But it was the smell of the poisoned water that was worse for Merry.

There were no other ships docked, and no sign of people in the town beyond. No gulls wheeled in the sky above the harbour, the silence still and oppressive, with no hint that anyone was left alive there. Dread settled into the pit of Merry's stomach as the captain steered *Hellcat* closer to the dock.

As her second in command handled the tiller, Captain Higgins came to stand beside Donna where she waited near the gangway with Merry and Ellen.

'Mistress Syphera, are you sure you want to get off here? It looks as if they fled in whatever ships and boats they had that would float,' she said, pointing to derelict ships on the dry docks. 'The rest must have fled overland, as it doesn't look like anyone is left here. If the water is poisoned as you say, it may not be safe to venture onto land. I'll be heading to Blackstone Harbour from here, and you are welcome to stay aboard.'

Donna gave a grim nod. 'Thank you, Captain Higgins. I think that would be wise. But I believe Merry and Ellen will still wish to disembark here.'

The captain turned to face them. 'Are you girls crazy? You would have to be, to want anything to do with this cursed place.' She waved a hand at the town, the stink a doom laden pall in the air above it. 'You'd be better off continuing on to Blackstone with the rest of your people.'

Merry wished she had the option of staying aboard. But she had to get to the Water focal point to have any hope of getting her next charm. If what Debra had said was true, and the Huntingdon people intended to use the portal at her grandmother's bookshop to invade Tirana, she had to get back there to renew the wards to stop them. She'd already lost time by being inveigled in the schemes of others since she'd arrived. She couldn't afford to lose more time by having to find another way to get to the Water focal point.

'We have no choice. We have to get off here,' she said.

'Very well, I will draw close enough for you to get to the dock and give you what supplies we can spare. If the poison is in the water, you can't risk drinking or eating anything from here until you get clear of the taint,' said Captain Higgins, misgiving etched on her face.

Within minutes, both Merry and Ellen carried a full water canteen and a small sack of food along with their packs.

'I wish we could give you more,' said the captain. 'But I need to keep enough on hand to feed the rest of us for the voyage to Blackstone.'

'You have been more than generous, Captain Higgins,' said Ellen. 'We thank you for your aid.' She clasped the captain's hands, while Merry said goodbye to Donna.

'Be careful out there,' said the Spirit mage. 'Whoever created this taint is a powerful Water mage. They could still be here, somewhere. You'll never make it home if you fall afoul of them.'

Merry grimaced at the thought. She did not need to find her way into even more trouble. Though trouble seemed to have a way of finding her ever since she landed in Tirana.

She straightened the makeshift mask Ellen had given her. The herbs stitched into the folds helped to mask some of the stench, but it was still strong enough to make her eyes water. She stepped gingerly onto the gangplank, the thought of falling and landing in the tainted water making her shudder as she crossed the plank. She did not breathe easily until she was safely on the dock.

Ellen stepped across just as carefully, while Sadie made the crossing in graceful bounds. They didn't wait to watch *Hellcat* sail out of the harbour. Conscious of Donna and many of the witches crowded at the railing watching on, Merry and her friends headed for the end of the dock and into the town itself.

Merry's stomach churned at the sight of rotten produce spilling from wagons as they passed through what appeared to be a loading area, and here and there she glimpsed the bloated bodies of dead dogs and horses, while the carcasses of chickens lay in the bottom of a wire pen.

She tore her gaze away from the sight, fixing them on the buildings to either side of the wide cobbled street that led away from the harbour. Many doors were open, but no sound came from within. There weren't even the sounds of insects; no flies buzzing over the dead animals.

It was eerie, but in a different way to the way the haunted enclave of Ralinin had been. She had no sense of spirits watching on, just the impression of a charnel house waiting to snare its next victim.

With that thought sitting uncomfortably in her stomach, Merry hurried through the empty streets as fast as she could go. Captain Higgins was right. This place was cursed. The sooner they got out of there the better.

The stench of rotting flesh dissipated as they cleared a large cluster of buildings and neared what appeared to be a large common area, free standing buildings lining one side. The cobbled street they had travelled on all the way from the harbour was now a dirt road that bisected the common. They had found no sign there was anyone left alive in the harbour town, and on the common the grass was churned up by wagon tracks and the tramping of many feet, indicating a mass exodus of those who had once lived there. The only patch of grass that remained intact was a section around a large well. Filled with misgiving, Merry wrapped her hands in cloth before touching the crank that drew the bucket out of the well's depths. The bucket was filled with tainted water, the shine visible to Merry long before she had it to the top and the sickly scent of it reached her nose.

'Can you see it?' Merry asked Ellen.

The healer shook her head, one hand stretched out above the bucket and the other on her heartstone pendant. 'I can't sense anything wrong with the water at all. If it wasn't for you telling me there is something wrong with it, I would think it fine to drink.'

Merry let the crank go, listening as the bucket filled with poisoned water fell back into the depths of the well. Unless they were Water witches, the townspeople would have been unaware the water was poisoned. How long had it taken, before the water had been suspected as the cause of the illness that had to have been sweeping through the town, and how much of a panic had that caused? From the chaos left in their wake, it was clear the people had fled in a hurry, household items left where they fell in the rush to flee the tainted water. As they moved towards the buildings on the other side of the common, Merry spotted a fabric doll, its once cream face smeared with mud, and could imagine the confused child being hurried along by its parents, the once treasured toy left behind.

She shook off the melancholy thought as they drew closer to what looked like a church. Ellen was a little way ahead of her and was standing near a low stone wall that ran down the other side of the church. The healer's shoulders shook, tears spilling down her cheeks as she twisted her head and looked at Merry.

Merry's gut clenched at her friend's grief-stricken

expression and she steeled herself to face the cause as she stepped closer and then peered over the wall.

A neat row of old graves filled the first half of the graveyard beside the church. Beyond that were what appeared to be fresh graves, the dirt raised above them. But behind that was a huge mound of dirt. Bouquets of wilting flowers were laid around the edges of the mound and Merry gasped, eyes wide as she realised what she was looking at.

A mass grave.

How many had died that the people here could no longer bury them individually? The panic these people must have felt would have been horrendous, to make them stop burying their dead individually and resort to a mass grave instead.

Sadie jumped onto the wall in front of Merry, gently butting her head into Merry's side. *There is nothing we can do to help the dead. It is clear many people survived the sickness and were able to flee this cursed town. We must do the same. Once we reach the Water focal point and find your charm, we will mourn those who lost their lives.*

Merry turned away from the graveyard, tears stinging her eyes as she reached out and grasped Ellen's hand. Sadie scouted ahead as they edged around the common and stepped back onto the dirt road that led inland. They kept their masks on until they were well clear of the poisoned harbour town, but the wind would occasionally blow the stench their way.

As with the common, the grass to either side of the

dirt road they now travelled on was trampled and churned up by the passage of those who had not been able to flee by sea. Belongings lay scattered among the corrugated wagon tracks. The chill wind continued to blow the occasional whiff of rot, but once the road curved around a large hill and the harbour town could no longer be seen, some of the tension seeped out of Merry's body, leaving her stiff and sore but relieved there was no longer any sign of poisoned water.

The road led them to a lush green valley nestled between two low hills, and they stopped to rest within a thicket of trees to eat a quick meal while Ellen checked their map.

'The Water focal point is a rock pool at the base of a waterfall,' she said. 'From the looks of it, it will take us at least a day to get there.'

A day of travel, plus however long it took Merry to find an appropriate charm and channel Water magic with it. Then they could get as far away from this province as possible. She only hoped the taint had not spread further than the harbour. They had limited supplies and would not last long if every source of water they came across was poisoned.

There were no birds nesting in the trees around them that she could see or hear, the valley even absent the buzzing of insects. She'd got used to the quiet of Tirana, with no traffic noise to disturb the peace, but this was quiet of a different kind. Eerie. Disturbing.

A shiver swept over her that had nothing to do with

the cool breeze and everything to do with the idea she and her friends could be the only ones left alive in the entire province.

The oat biscuits they'd been given on *Hellcat* tasted like dust in her mouth, but she forced herself to chew and swallow, washing it down with a few sips of water to conserve her supply. Then she stood, eager to get moving again.

They spent a quiet night in a wooden hut that looked to have been well used by travellers over the years, though there was no sign those who had fled had stopped to use it. No doubt their panic had them continuing on through the night, desperate to get away from the tainted water as fast as possible. Though Merry and her friends were just as eager to complete their journey, they were all still tired after the escape from Greystone and did not want to risk stumbling around in the dark with only the light of Merry's staff to lead the way. They were up at dawn to continue their trek, not wanting to waste a moment of daylight.

Despite the gloomy circumstance they were currently facing, as her muscles warmed up Merry found it easier going than when she had first arrived in Tirana. Thanks to the many days she had spent walking, she was fitter than she had ever been. Her food had been simpler than what she'd eaten back home, too, not that she'd been a huge fan of junk food. But her mouth watered at the thought of biting into a huge burger from her favourite takeaway place. Or slurping down an icy cold beer while watching a movie.

When she did finally get home, she was not going to take for granted the simple pleasure to be found in just being clean, well fed and not in fear for her life.

If she got home.

No. She couldn't think like that. She had managed to get the first two charms she needed, even if each challenge had tested her in ways she was sure would affect her forever. She would get the last three as well, no matter what Tirana threw at her.

Hours later, once they crested the top of yet another sloping valley, Merry could not stifle a groan of dismay at what she saw on the other side. The waterfall was magnificent, streams of water spilling over the edge of a cliff to land with dramatic flair into the rock pool below.

The rock pool shone with a familiar green and blue taint.

'It's poisoned. The focal point,' said Ellen, voice strained.

Merry turned to the healer, eyebrows raised. 'You can see it?'

'Yes.' Ellen's face was pale as she placed a hand against her stomach. 'It's horrible. Looking at it makes me want to retch.'

Merry winced. If Ellen, who had no Water magic, could see the taint then it had to be even worse here than it had been back at the harbour town.

I can also see it. Sadie's tail swished backwards and forwards, her whiskers twitching. *And smell it. I will remain here, while the two of you find your charm.*

Merry relayed Sadie's words to Ellen, and then the two of them replaced their masks and started walking towards the rock pool. The closer they got, the more Merry feared she would never find the charm she needed. The ground between them was littered with the carcasses of birds, but the smell of their rotting flesh paled in comparison with the stench coming from the rock pool. The herbs Ellen had sprinkled inside the mask was no match for it. Her eyes watered as Merry fought to remember to breathe through her mouth and not her nose as she and Ellen drew closer.

It wasn't until she was almost at the edge of the rock pool that she realised something was missing.

When she had approached the Air and Earth focal points, a thrum of magic resonated in the air around her. Here the only thing she could feel was a bad case of pins and needles all over her body.

She could have put it down to her not actually having Water magic, but she had definitely felt the buzz when she had flung her deluge of sea water at the militia and renegade mages when they'd been fleeing them in the cove. While on board *Hellcat*, she and the Water witches were the only ones to sense the taint both in the water around the ship and on the birds that had fallen from the sky.

As the stench emanating from the rock pool got so

bad she could not get any closer to it without throwing up, Merry stopped and put her back to it, indicating for Ellen to do the same.

'Are you sure the rock pool is the focal point? I can't sense any Water magic coming from it at all. Could it have been poisoned along with the water?'

Ellen shook her head. 'That shouldn't even be possible. Elemental magic forms the backbone of Tirana. Without it, the land would wither and die. We need all five elements to retain the balance.'

'I can't sense any Water magic.' She reached out with her Earth magic but all she could sense was the taint. It was slimy and insidious in her mind, as if it was just waiting for her to allow it access so it could stain her irrevocably. She shuddered at the thought and drew her senses back.

'You used Water magic back at the cove, when we were under attack, and when the enforcers tried to kidnap you on *Hellcat*.'

Merry grimaced as she said, 'There was no poisoned water either of those times, and I could feel the magic of the element. But here there is nothing.' She indicated back to the rock pool. 'It's even smothering my sense of Earth.'

Ellen frowned as she twisted around and stared at the rock pool. 'It's not blocking my Earth abilities, such as they are. Maybe yours is affected because you are stronger than me. Either way, we need to find the source of the taint. It may be magical in nature, but it is still just a poison. If we can find the antidote, we can stop it from spreading further and then find a way to cure it. Maybe if we can do that, the Water focal point will recover.'

Ellen was a healer, making it normal for her to think in terms of cures. But she worked with regular illness. Merry didn't think curing the taint would be as simple as that, but they had to try.

'Any idea where we can find the source?'

'We follow the water.' Ellen turned around and pointed to the waterfall. Now that they were so close, Merry could see the water that crashed over the edge of the cliff and into the rock pool also carried the blue green glow of the taint, though it was not as bright as the water within the rockpool itself. Perhaps that was because the rock pool acted as a reservoir?

Though it would be overflowing if that was the case, so there had to be an underground passage some of the water escaped through. That thought did not sit easily with Merry, as she could imagine the poison travelling through the ground beneath her feet. That must have been how the well back at the harbour town had been infected.

They walked back to where Sadie waited for them, and the three of them set off up a steep track that led to the top of the hill that housed the waterfall. All Merry's thoughts of being fit faded as the climb set her leg and back muscles burning. Sweat coated her body, even as her mouth dried out from all her gasping for air. She couldn't afford to stop and have a drink, with no idea how far they would have to travel before they found good water and could refill their skins.

Her lungs were burning, and her entire body shaking, by the time she reached the top of the hill and could see the sparkling blue green water of the river that fed the waterfall. It was fast flowing and wide, and though looking at it increased her thirst, the taint made her stomach churn.

Still, the stench was not as strong here as it had been down near the rock pool. It was overshadowed by the smell of rot from carcasses of sheep and cattle that appeared to have been poisoned a number of days ago. She and her friends gave the bodies of the dead livestock a wide berth as they followed the river upstream, back towards the harbour town. As they walked, Merry could still see the gleam on the water but it was not as bright as it had been closer to the waterfall, or in the rock pool itself.

The sun was dipping low by the time they reached a fork in the river, one section continuing on to the coast, while the other headed further inland.

'Which way do we go now?' asked Ellen. 'I can't see the taint anymore.'

'It's brighter that way,' said Merry, pointing to the inland fork.

'Then we go that way, I guess.'

They set off along the new section of the river, Merry sure they had to be getting closer to the source as the taint became increasingly brighter. Of course, she still had no idea how they were going to find an antidote or cure for whatever magical poison had been unleashed here.

The longer they walked, the worse Merry's nausea grew, and Ellen was similarly afflicted. Not even Sadie was immune, though she didn't appear to be as hard hit. They took a short break so Ellen could refresh the herbs sewn into their masks, but even with the extra zing of her magically enhanced herbs, the smell was still enough to make Merry retch anytime she forgot to breathe through her mouth.

She wanted nothing more than to turn in the other direction and get as far away from the water as possible, but instead forced herself to keep going. The taint was a miasma that coated everything it touched in the sickly blue green sheen. The banks of the river gave off an eerie light. They kept as close as they could stomach as they followed the winding river through rolling hills and lush green valleys, but the grass near the edge of the river was beginning to rot, adding to the overall stench.

The land farther back from the river was as yet untouched and should have been filled with grazing animals. They found more huts that looked to have been used by shepherds to tend to their flocks but, other than a couple dead sheep, there were no animals to be seen. Like in the harbour town, the birds and then the insects had fled for safer pastures.

They crested a steep hill, with the river on their

right, and a steep cliff rising to their left. Merry shaded her eyes from the late afternoon sun as she looked ahead.

A grey blocky structure spanned the river a short distance away. The water splashed against it, staining the grey stone. The structure was tall, and extended on the left side of the river, butting up against the base of the cliff, while what appeared to be buildings were on top of it.

'It's the Marshland Dam,' said Ellen, her voice nasal as she consulted her map, no doubt from trying not to breathe in any more of the stench than she had to.

They quickened their pace, angling closer to the river to get to the road that ran towards the dam. There was a wide door that led to a ramp inside the wall, and despite their weary muscles and aching lungs, they hurried to the top and found themselves on a road that led through the buildings on top of the dam. There was a low wall on either side of the road, and Merry rushed over to look at what lay beyond.

The land on this side was flatter, a mix of greens, with waterways dotted throughout. They were clear waterways from the look of it. Merry leaned over the edge and saw untainted grassland at the base of the dam wall.

'The dam has stopped the poison from spreading to the other side,' she said as Ellen came over and also peered over the wall.

Sadie sprang up onto the wall and peered into the

distance. *This part of the province was once a boggy marsh. A former Lord Marshland had the dam built to triple the size of arable land and make his province more profitable.*

The dam had saved two thirds of the province from whatever was poisoning the water on this side. From the high vantage point, Merry could see green rolling lands that led to a forest that spread as far as she could see, with birds wheeling in the air above. The sense of normality was surreal after the lifelessness of what they had encountered so far. The feel of the taint was so strong here, the urge to retch almost overwhelming, and she was looking out over land so far untouched.

'The poison is definitely being spread by the water, then,' said Ellen. 'But we still haven't found the source.'

Merry wasn't so sure about that. Hers arms were prickling, like a thousand ants biting into her. She'd felt a similar sensation when they had been at the rock pool but had been too distracted by the stench and slimy presence in her mind to register it properly.

'There is something very wrong here.' She forced herself to focus on the feel of the taint, head cocked to the side, holding her breath to block out the stench. 'It's coming from down there.' She pointed at the road ahead of them, to where the squat buildings crouched on the sides of the road across the dam wall.

'Inside the dam itself?' Ellen frowned. 'But there's no water in there. How would it have spread to the rock pool from here?'

'I think there are two sources of the taint,' said

Merry, thinking it out as she spoke. 'One in the rock pool, and one here.' It made sense, matching up to what she felt in both places. 'If we find whatever it is inside the dam that I can sense, and discover a way to neutralise it, then we can do the same thing back at the rock pool.'

She hoped.

All this was just guessing based on how the taint made her feel.

'So how do we get inside?' Ellen asked.

Merry scanned the buildings. 'Maybe there's a way inside through one of the these.' They started forward, Sadie walking along the wall beside them, towards the buildings.

A shiver swept over Merry as three people stepped out of a building on the left.

Duck.

At Sadie's mental shout Merry grabbed Ellen's arms and pulled her down. A split second later, a plume of fire shot through the air above them.

Damn.

Merry scrambled backward, pulling Ellen with her. Was this the Fire mage from the cove or another magic user? Could he have got here before them? The overland route was supposed to take four days.

A large group of people spilled out of the building dressed in the familiar uniform of the militia from Greystone, an orange robed mage in their midst, but Merry had no time to ponder their presence here in

Marshland or determine if this was the mage she had fought before. More fire streaked their way.

Merry's mind raced for how to counter the mage's magic. She'd used the ocean to extinguish fireballs back in the cove, but the water here was bad. She did not want to risk any of it landing on her or her friends, even if she could stomach the thought of attempting to touch it with her mind. Besides, she'd sensed no magic in the water at all since the taint had first appeared while they were on *Hellcat*.

She briefly considered using her Earth magic to cause a quake, but the thought of destroying the dam, letting the water spill through to the untainted land on the other side did not sit well with her.

That left Air.

She gripped her staff and flung up a wall of air as the fireball streaked towards them. Then she pushed it back, sending the mage and militia running for cover. The Fire mage may be able to create and control fire, but clearly had no aptitude for Air. This was lucky for her and the others.

They retreated to the ramp and sprinted towards the base of the dam wall. Once they reached the ground, Merry desperately scanned the terrain. For once fear helped to drown out the stench from the taint. They couldn't go closer to the river, so they headed for the base of the cliffs as fast as they could go. Shouts came from the ramp and Merry knew they would not make it to the cliff let alone be able to find a place to hide before their attackers reached the ground and spotted them.

'Stop,' she called out to Ellen. The healer froze, fear etched on her face, eyes wide.

Merry didn't have time to explain her plan. 'Up against the wall,' she said, suiting her actions to her words and reaching out to grasp her friend's arm. Merry took a deep breath, willing the thudding of her heart to ease, as she started up her litany. *Do not see us. Do not hear us.*

Sadie slunk in beside her, fur soft against Merry's ankle.

Her heart gave a jolt as the Fire mage and the militia appeared in her periphery, but she resisted the urge to move. She felt Ellen stiffen beside her and suck in a shallow breath.

Do not see us. Do not hear us.

'Spread out. They can't have gone far,' called out the mage as he strode to almost within reach. His brow was creased, fists clenched at his sides as he scanned the grassy hills in the distance.

The militia followed his command and combed the area, some jogging over to the base of the cliffs and others the nearest hills. All the while, Merry continued her litany.

Her muscles cramped from staying still for so long, but she didn't dare move. At one time the mage turned to face them, and she could have sworn he was looking directly at her. If he was like her, and could sense when someone nearby was performing magic, then they were in trouble.

She tried to project an image of the grey wall, willing him to see nothing else, and almost gave a sigh when he finally turned away.

Eventually the searching militiamen returned and reported their failure.

'Damn it.' The mage slammed one hand against the wall so close to Merry that she felt the wind stirred by its passage. Then he strode back to the doorway that led to the ramp, orange robe flapping at his heels, calling out orders for the militia to increase their patrols, and soon disappeared from view.

Merry waited for a long moment after the last of the militia had followed in his wake before she dared move, but she did not stop the litany repeating in her mind.

She held a finger to her lip, indicating for Ellen to remain silent, and then pointed towards the base of the cliff. They moved slowly, and it was not until they were wedged in the corner made where the wall was seamlessly joined to the cliff face that Merry took her first easy breath.

'We have to go back to the rock pool,' she said. 'To see if I can figure out how to remove whatever is poisoning the water there.'

Ellen shook her head. 'We have barely any water left, and not much food. What if you can't fix the water? We need to get across this wall and find more supplies before you're too weak to use your magic to hide us.'

Merry didn't like it, but knew Ellen was right. They'd gone through most of the water Captain Higgins had given them just getting this far. To walk all the way back to the rock pool would take what they had left, leaving them with none if she couldn't fix the poison.

She knew nothing about the poison; only that it was magical in nature.

She didn't know what she was doing, when it came to magic. She was crazy to think she'd even have a chance of fixing that taint.

From what I understand, the Lord Marshland who built the dam was a strong Water mage. There is a chance his descendants will also have Water magic. This is their province, after all. If we tell them what is happening, the current lord may be able to help.

Merry told Ellen what Sadie had suggested.

'Master Roberts said Marshland is now ruled by Lady Beatrice Marsh,' said Ellen.

'Okay then, we see if we can find this Lady Beatrice and hope she knows how to treat magically poisoned water.'

Merry clasped Ellen's hand and started up her litany once more as they crept along the dam wall, slowly making for the road. They would have to travel back to where the river had forked and cross to the other side. She just wished she didn't feel as if they were running from one problem straight to another one.

They kept to the shadows cast by trees lining a well-trodden dirt path. It had taken them three hours to work their way to the other side of the river, crossing a stone bridge. Now they edged closer to the dam wall, sticking to the tree line as they followed the path when it skirted the river and got them closer to the wall. As they walked, they found evidence that others had travelled this way recently, giving them hope there would be a way to get to the untainted half of Marshland Province.

Soon they would have to leave the relative security of the tree line, but as the afternoon was waning, Merry hoped the shadows of dusk would be enough to shield them from the eyes of the militia on top of the dam wall. Unlike when they had approached it before, she could see figures walking around, presumably on guard now they knew someone was in the area.

As dusk came, flickering lights flared to life on top of the dam wall, torches from the look of it. Merry wished she and Ellen could chance a light, as they stumbled their way over tree roots. They couldn't risk it and relied on Sadie's keen eyesight to lead them around obstacles.

Staff gripped in one hand, Merry was still keeping her mental litany going in her head, to avoid being seen or heard, but could feel her strength waning. For all she knew, she was focusing on the litany for no reason, her magic no longer strong enough to hide them. Their passage was frustratingly slow, and as the path curved away from the river and closer to the dam wall, she hoped it wouldn't be necessary to hide much longer.

Sadie turned the corner first, a wave of horror flowing through the bond with Merry the second she was out of sight. *Oh no.*

Merry hurried around the corner, and then threw a hand over her mouth to stifle her instinctive scream.

Bodies lay beside the path, the sheen from the taint visible on the skin exposed by their clothing. There were five of them, huddled together; a man, woman, and three children. It was a family, by the look of it, the arms of the parents wrapped around the children lying between them.

Tears pricked Merry's eyes and she dashed at them with her hand. Ellen hurried forward, and Merry caught her arm. 'Don't touch them. They've been poisoned.'

'Who could do such a thing?' Ellen's low cry was

filled with anguish. 'Poison children.' She fell to her knees a short distance from the bodies, tears streaming down her cheeks.

'I don't know.' Whoever had made this magical taint, and unleashed it on the unsuspecting people of Marshland, was a monster.

'I need a light,' said Ellen, voice choked with grief.

Merry scanned the dam wall. The corner had turned them away slightly, meaning they were out of sight from the top and she couldn't see any sign of windows on the wall itself. She moved closer to Ellen, willing her staff to glow.

In the soft light from Merry's staff, Ellen leaned over the body of the woman. 'She hasn't been dead long. A day at most.' She touched her chest, where her heart-stone pendant lay hidden by the bodice of her dress. 'It's hard to pinpoint the true cause of death, without a more thorough examination, but it appears her internal organs all shut down at once. Just like the birds on *Hellcat.*' Ellen cast a despairing glance over the other bodies. 'They all died the same way.'

Merry shuddered. What a horrible way to die.

Ellen got to her feet and wiped her tears away with jerky movements. Then she faced Merry, chin jutting forward and a militant light in her eyes. 'They have to be stopped. We need to figure out how to get rid of the taint, and then we find who did this and make them pay.'

Staring at the bodies, the way the parents had curled themselves around their children, Merry wished for nothing more than to be able to make the person or people responsible pay. To have any hope of doing that, they needed to get to the other side of the dam wall and find supplies, allies, something that would help them with the first step.

'We need to go,' she said, her own voice as choked up as Ellen's, 'before the militia comes looking for us.'

'We can't just leave them like this.' Ellen shook her head, fresh tears gleaming in her eyes.

'We have nothing to bury them with, and we can't be sure the taint won't spread to us if we touch their bodies. We'll come back, I promise, once we find help.'

Ellen gave a nod, and they set off. Merry cast one last look at the dead family before following her friend, wishing it didn't feel like abandoning them. It wasn't right, to leave them like that, but they had no choice.

The path curved inwards a short distance beyond the spot where the family had died, and Merry had to put out the light of her staff as they would once again be visible to those on top of the dam wall.

Noise came ahead of them, voices, and Sadie stiffened, casting a look back at Merry. *Wait here. I will investigate.* The little cat bounded through the shadows, her black coat making her almost invisible.

Seconds later, she reappeared at Merry's side, making her jump. *A dozen militia are guarding the path that leads around the edge of the dam wall, and they have an Earth mage with them.*

Is there another way we can get past them? What about if I used my invisibility spell?

They have the entire path blocked, and an Earth mage may be able to sense us, even if you were strong enough to render us invisible once more. We cannot risk it.

Merry grimaced as she leaned in close to Ellen and told her what Sadie had said.

As silently as they could, they began to retrace their steps, gazes averted as they passed the dead family. All of this, and they had nothing to show for it. Worse than nothing. They had used up valuable time and energy to get to this point, only to have to turn around.

Now what were they supposed to do?

They were trapped in a land that was tainted with a poison so virulent it killed all it touched. They had hardly any water or food left, and the only way to untainted land was blocked by the enemy.

Merry had never felt so hopeless as she did at that point.

They trudged on through the night, not stopping to rest until they were well away from the dam. Then, in the glow of Merry's staff, they stared at the map. Marshland Province was shaped like a teardrop. The section they were in jutted out at the top, with the steep cliffs to either side of the river that flowed into the larger section. With the dam wall crossing the river, and reaching to both sides of the cliffs, and the dam itself guarded by militia and mages, there was no way through.

'Maybe we can get past the poison. Find a boat back at the harbour so we can follow the coastline until we reach untainted land.' Ellen smoothed the map before folding it up and replacing it in her pack, indecision on her face.

'The townspeople took everything that could float and got out of here, leaving the rest to attempt the path around the dam.' That path had led to the death of some of them. They'd found signs of more bodies, hastily buried, as they had fled the militia.

Merry pulled her thoughts from wondering how many hadn't made it to safety. 'The only boats left will be ones that wouldn't stay afloat.' She remembered seeing a jumble of wrecks on the rocky ground at one end of the harbour.

'You have Earth magic. Maybe you could fix one of them. With your Air magic, you could speed up our passage, get us to the other side of Marshland faster.'

Merry frowned, imagining trying to keep a leaky boat afloat with one spell, while commanding the wind to blow them faster with another. The way she felt now, as though even a gentle wind would knock her over, made her doubt she could manage one spell let alone two for however long it would take to get clear of the taint. But what choice did they have? They couldn't stay there.

First, you must both rest. Sadie gave a shake, ears twitching. *Neither of you will be able to use your magic to best effect if you are exhausted.*

The familiar was right. They ate a meagre meal with the rest of their supplies and sipped sparingly of what water they had left, Sadie delicately lapping water from Merry's cupped hands. Then they settled in to spend a restless night curled up in the underbrush. Merry tossed on the hard ground, feeling the jab of rocks and twigs in each position she tried. She eventually managed to fall asleep, conscious of the silhouette of Sadie as she kept watch.

Wake! Someone is coming.

The cat's mental shout seemed to come seconds after Merry had closed her eyes. She sat up, disoriented. It was still dark, the moon glinting through gaps in the tree branches above her head as she leaned over and shook Ellen to wake her. She could just see the sheen of her friend's eyes as she whispered news of Sadie's alarm. Then they waited, silent, unmoving. Listening. Noises drifted on the wind, the sound of people tramping over twigs and dead leaves. Coming closer.

No voices, so whoever was coming their way was keeping silent. Only the sound of their passage signalled their presence.

As quietly as she could, Merry got to her feet, one hand clasping her staff, the other reaching for her pack. She stumbled, a wave of dizziness swamping her, and would have fallen if not for her staff. She was bone tired, weak from lack of food and water as well as sleep. Her lips were dry, throat parched, and she'd kill for a bottle of cold water to quench her thirst.

She reached out with her magic, trying to sense who the people were, but pain stabbed her head at the attempt. So, no invisibility spell. They would just have to stay as still and quiet as possible and hope that whoever was out there passed them by. The odds they were friendly did not seem high in a place where the taint was so entrenched. The only life they'd seen so far had been the militia from Greystone and renegade mages. This could be a search party, out hunting for Merry and her friends.

The noises receded, and Merry fought the urge to sag in relief against the tree at her back. They were in no condition to protect themselves.

She waited a long moment, ears straining for any sound.

Sadie, have they gone?

The little cat was best suited to scouting out trouble. Her keen eyesight and hearing meant she could discern what human senses could not.

Sadie?

Merry's pulse sped up. Why hadn't the familiar responded? She couldn't be out of range in such a short space of time.

Merry squinted her eyes and fought to pierce the shadows, seeking a darker shape low to the ground. Nothing. All she could see was shadowy tree trunks and bushes. No sign of the little cat.

A loud thud came to her left, and Merry spun around to see Ellen slumped on the ground. She tried to move towards her friend, but her limbs didn't obey. She couldn't move. She tried to yell, but though her mouth opened no sound came out.

As panic at being frozen in place hit and a painful buzz set up in her head, she fought to lift a hand to her temple, only to be swamped with blackness. She felt herself falling. She hit the ground, hard, the pain of her landing muted by the pained buzz in her head. It drowned out thought and feelings. She lay on her side, eyes open but unable to move as flickering light flared in the trees just beyond their makeshift camp. Figures stepped forward, the light from the burning brand burnishing the red robes of the two people at the front.

A hand gripped Merry's arm and she was rolled onto her back, staring up in horror at the two people looming over her.

Kassandra Piermont and her brother, Karl.

Merry was conscious of more people standing behind them, but all her attention was focused on the two rogue enforcers. What were they doing here?

She was pulled to her feet, her hands tied behind her back, while Ellen was treated similarly. She tried to speak, to ask what they were going to do with them, but no words would form. Whatever had been done to immobilise them had robbed her of speech. The painful buzz was still in her head, but it lessened slightly as she was tugged forward.

She stumbled and then righted herself, relieved to

have regained use of her legs. But other than being able to breathe and blink, the rest of her body felt like something that did not belong to her. She was marched through the trees to the path, where she found Sadie slung over the shoulder of a man in a familiar militia uniform, but not from Greystone.

This was the silver and black of Lord Andel's men.

Horrified as she was to see evidence of the renegade lord working with the rogue enforcers, Merry's immediate concern was the little black cat. She held her breath until she saw the eyes slowly blink. She was alive; immobilised by whatever had Merry and Ellen half paralysed, and somehow cut off from telepathic communication.

They were shoved along the path by more men wearing the uniform of Lord Andel's militia. Merry stumbled, falling to her knees, and was roughly pulled to her feet.

Her limbs shook, throat so parched she wouldn't have been able to call for help even if her vocal cords were working properly. She was dizzy, and so very tired it was hard to think. Her breathing was fast, and she could feel her heart pounding in her chest. It became too much effort to lift her foot for the next step when the man holding on to the rope ahead of her gave a tug. She stumbled and fell to the ground, landing on her side with a thud that jarred every bone in her body.

She had no energy to be grateful for the paralysis

that had clearly spared her from what should have been a painful experience, and simply lay there as the militiaman continued to pull on the rope. It was no use. She couldn't move even if she wanted to.

Someone leaned over her, and she slowly blinked, working to clear her vision. All she could see was a green blur. Then someone placed a hand on her forehead and warmth flooded her body.

'She's severely dehydrated. Same as the other one. They need water and time for their bodies to recover.' The voice was female, cool and impersonal.

'Do what you have to and get them moving again.' This voice was male, hard edged. 'We're wasting time.'

More warmth flooded Merry and some of the dizziness receded, though her throat was still dry enough to use as sandpaper. She was dragged to her feet, and she swayed a little until she got her balance back.

To the left, a woman in a green robe was kneeling beside Ellen. Soon her friend was also standing and the woman who had treated them stood back.

'It's a short term fix,' she said. 'Without proper fluids, they won't last long.'

'Just as long as they last until we get to the dam,' said the male.

Karl. That was his name.

Some of the fog had left her brain with whatever the woman, the Earth mage, had done to her. It was enough to realise the rogue enforcer had no care for their wellbeing. While the Earth mage might have healing skills, her emotionless voice was a far cry from Ellen's calm and soothing manner with those in need of healing.

Red flared in the corner of Merry's eye, and then Kassandra was standing in front of her. Merry winced in anticipation, expecting the enforcer to lash out. But instead she held a water skin up to her mouth.

'Drink,' she said, voice low, brows lowered and the skin round her eyes tight.

She tipped the skin and Merry opened her mouth, stifling a moan as precious water slipped down her throat and soothed some of the dryness. She hadn't realised just how thirsty she was until that moment. She wanted to wallow in the water, cover herself in it.

All too soon Kassandra stepped back. Merry tried to lift her arms to grab the water skin back, but her upper body was still frozen. She could only watch as the enforcer moved to the left and repeated the process with Ellen and then Sadie. She could not begrudge her friends a drink, though she couldn't tear her gaze away from the water skin, hoping the enforcer would return to her with it.

'What are you doing?' Karl strode to his sister's side and tore the water skin from her hand.

'They needed water,' she said meekly, lowering her head.

'I'm in charge of this mission, not you,' he said, looming over her.

Kassandra flinched. 'I'm sorry. I know you're in a hurry. I thought they would go faster if they had something to drink.'

'If they don't keep up, we drag them. No more water.'

Kassandra gave a nod and then stepped away, back straight, not looking back, as the men holding the ropes gave them a tug.

Merry and Ellen shared a glance as they were tugged along the path. From her expression, Merry was sure her friend was wondering the same thing she was. What the hell had just happened? From the looks of it, Kassandra was scared of her brother. This was the brother she had ruined her position with the guild for by helping him flee before he could be questioned.

He was clearly working with Lord Andel, and he'd said he was in charge of the mission, which put him in charge of the Earth mage as well. What that mission was, she was sure had something to do with the poisoned water and the force who had taken control of the dam wall.

Her thoughts were coming faster now, the water Kassandra had given her helping even more than whatever it was the mage had done. But she was still weak. She attempted to reach her magic, to sense around the area, and the immediate ache in her head made her stop. So, still no magic.

She would have to figure out how she and the others could escape the old fashioned way.

Only, surrounded by the enemy, tied up and with her

upper body still numb, was not the best position to be in to pull off a miraculous escape. She would have to bide her time and wait until either she regained the ability to use her magic or their captors eased up on their restrictions.

Her decision to wait was tested as they tramped through the night, back towards the dam. The closer she got, the worse grew her nausea. Now it had nothing to do with dehydration or lack of food. It was all the taint, and she couldn't even use her hands to cover her face or retrieve the mask Ellen had made to block out the stench. Her head reeled and she fought the urge to retch, barely able to focus on keeping upright, let alone plan an escape as they neared the dam.

It was a relief when they finally reached the dam wall and moved into an aperture the same as the one on the other side of the river. Her legs shook as she was tugged up the ramp, the stone wall on either side working to shield her somewhat from the stench of the water.

She gingerly stretched out her senses, relieved when it produced only a dull ache as she concentrated on the feel of the stone beneath her feet. Concentrating on that helped to block out the stench even more, which was especially good as the taint strengthened when she was shoved into one of the buildings and forced down a set of stone steps into the depths of the dam itself.

Torchlight flickered off the stone walls to either side of her, and as they were marched inexorably downward

Merry hoped she had not taken her last glimpse of the sky.

They were surrounded by enemies; rendered powerless.

Could her life get any worse?

CHAPTER 9

*M*erry was jerked to a stop, a hard tug on the rope threatening to send her tumbling onto the stone floor. She caught herself at the last second and glared at the guard who was in charge of her. With stone on all sides of her, blocking out the worst of the taint, she was feeling much more alert now. Lack of food and water meant she wasn't ready to fight back, not when they were outnumbered so badly and even thinking about magic made the pounding in her head ten times worse, but she was ready to exploit any non-magical avenue she and her friends could use to escape.

As they spilled into a large space filled with wide grey pipes overhead, Merry ran her gaze around in hope of finding something that would help them get the better of their captors. Instead, she stiffened at the sight of over a dozen militia and two mages. One of the mages wore a purple robe, the other was the Fire mage she had gone up against hours earlier. Tension thrummed through her. If he happened to throw a fire-ball her way now, she had nothing to deflect it with. Even more concerning, neither he nor the Spirit mage were the ones she had faced in Greystone.

How many renegades did Lord Andel have working for him? From the subservient way the Greystone militia reacted to the arrival of those from Andelmine, there was little doubt who was in charge.

A large smokeless fire was in the centre of the cavernous space, the flames blue and white and absent the crackling Merry associated with fire. Piles of bedding were set up in neat rows on one side of the magical blaze, as well as a number of packs, while boxes and barrels of supplies and the makings of a camp kitchen were on the other side. The comprehensive set up suggested people had been staying inside the dam for some time.

Karl called over the Spirit mage and then pointed at Kassandra. 'You need to break her oath to the guild. Now.'

Kassandra gasped and he rounded on her, his expression harder than the rock at Merry's back. 'The guild has made you soft.' He pointed at the water skin attached to her belt; the one she had allowed Merry and her friends to drink from. 'I need to know I can trust you.'

'Of course you can trust me,' she said, her face pale.

'You're my brother. I would never do anything to hurt you.'

A cruel twist to his mouth, he shifted to point at Ellen. 'Kill her.'

Kassandra reeled back, a hand going to her mouth as he leaned closer. 'Use your power and crush her spine.'

Merry reached into herself, seeking her magic, fear blotting out the pounding in her temples as Kassandra turned to face her friend. She would not let the enforcer hurt Ellen. Her magic sluggishly answered her call, weakened by deprivation just as her body was. She focused on the air around her, willing it to form into a force capable of slamming both Karl and Kassandra against the wall. She had no idea if it would work but she had to try.

A soft breeze stirred her hair. It was nowhere near strong enough to save Ellen.

Merry dug as deep as she could, silently screaming for her magic to respond, determined to throw every last scrap of her energy into creating a gale.

The Earth mage stepped closer and placed a hand on Merry's arm, the buzz in her head returning and smothering the tiny spark of magic. She fought to break free, but could do nothing, not even scream out loud as Kassandra pointed at Ellen.

The enforcer's hand shook and there was a grimace on her face.

No one else moved. No one said anything.

After a long moment Kassandra's shoulders slumped,

and she lowered her hand. 'I can't do it. I can't use my magic to harm another unless it is in self-defence or to apprehend them for the guild.'

'Stupid guild and their stupid rules,' sneered Karl. 'They've got you so tied up in knots with their oath that when the time comes to defend yourself you will only get yourself killed. I can't trust you until I know they no longer have a hold on you.'

He turned away from his sister and faced the Spirit mage once more. 'Well, what are you waiting for?'

The mage stiffened, a wary expression on his face. 'I am afraid I cannot do that.'

Karl's face was suffused with red. 'You will do exactly what I tell you to do,' he said as he raised his fist. 'Or I will squeeze your brain until it pops.'

The mage held his hands up in front of him. 'It's not that I don't want to. I can't. We have no more heart-stones. Some witch with purple hair joined forces with the Singers and chased Lord Andel and his men out of the mountain, sealing it off with magic. Word is the witch even killed Fowler. Lord Andel was lucky to escape with his life.'

With a roar, Karl turned around and pointed a clenched fist at Merry. She was yanked off her feet, the invisible force that had hold of her the only thing keeping her from slamming into the ground.

'Karl, what are you doing?'

He ignored Kassandra's shout, waving his other hand and sending his sister reeling back as he pulled Merry closer to a large barrel. With a flick of his wrist, the lid came off and clanged to the ground. She had a split second to see the gleam of liquid inside the barrel before she was jerked forward, her body bending so her head was suspended over the barrel.

Merry struggled to get free, terrified she was going to be infected by poisoned water, and have all her organs fail like those of the family that had died trying to escape. She closed her eyes and held her breath as her head was tipped into the barrel, even though she knew it would do no good.

Her relief at finding the barrel was filled with untainted water was fleeting as it filled her nose. She was flung around, like flotsam in a whirlpool, stomach churning with the force she was undergoing.

Her breath ran out, the burning in her lungs intensifying. The need to breathe grew ever more urgent. Eventually she could not resist, opening her mouth and choking as water flooded her throat.

Was he intending to drown her?

Then she was pulled from the barrel, retching up water, hair plastered around her face as she was dropped to the ground. She coughed as her lungs fought to get air, sagging weakly against the barrel she had been mercilessly dunked in, eyes closed, body shuddering.

A hard tug on her hair elicited tears as she was dragged to her feet. She opened her eyes to find Karl looming over her, a wet clump of brown tinged purple hair twisted around his fist.

'You ruin everything you touch,' he growled as he used his hold on her hair to throw her to the ground.

He stood over her, chest heaving, fists raised as a gust of wind whipped through the room and lashed her over and over again. She was still paralysed from whatever the Earth mage had done to her, and could do nothing to protect herself, but some of the numbness had worn off. Her body shuddered at each ice cold lash.

'Karl, stop. What are you doing?' Kassandra cried out. 'You said we need her alive.'

The wind lashed Merry several more times before it finally stopped and she lay on the cold floor, a sodden mess, shivering and holding back sobs. With the numbness fading, she now felt each bruise and scrape gained since they'd been captured, a deep ache settling in. She forced down the pain to focus on her enemy.

Kassandra stood in front of Karl, fear etched on her face but her back straight. 'You said we can use her against the guild. We can't do that if she's dead.'

For a long moment, Karl glared at his sister, before storming off. 'Get them locked up somewhere secure,' he called without looking back.

Merry sagged on the floor. The buzz was gone from her head, and she realised she could move again, but she was exhausted, mentally and physically. She could do nothing as one of the militia guards' untied her hands, picked her up and slung her over his shoulder.

It wasn't until she was laid down on a cold, hard surface, that she dared try to move.

Air hissed through her teeth at the fresh wave of pain that flared throughout her entire body.

'Stay still.' Ellen kneeled beside her, hands rested against Merry's head. Warmth flooded through her, far gentler and less invasive than when the mage had done whatever it had been to give them energy for the forced march back to the dam.

Still, as her shivers ceased, Merry knew it would not be enough. Now that some of the pain racking her body had eased, her senses were overwhelmed by the stench of tainted water. The stench was almost as strong as when she had been standing near the rock pool. This time when she retched it had everything to do with nausea roiling in her belly and not the water she had recently swallowed.

It took every ounce of self-control she had left to enable her to sit up and open her eyes, to look upon what fresh hell they had landed in.

The tiny room was dark and dank, with a nest of pipes criss-crossing the low ceiling. She would have to watch herself when she stood up to avoid banging her head on a pipe. They had been left with a small lantern, though the light it offered was dim and she had to wonder how long the oil in it would last and when they would be plunged into complete darkness.

Ellen was crouched over Sadie, hands on the black cat's side.

'Is she okay?' Merry got to her knees, bracing herself against the wall when the room spun at the movement, and then slowly made her way over to them.

'The mage used a nerve blocking spell to paralyse her, same as she did to us. It's meant to be used to stop pain and immobilise the patient while performing delicate healing, not to freeze people.' Her tone was affronted at this misuse of healing magic. 'I was able to reverse the effects on you and me, with the help of my heartstone. A cat's physiology is different from ours. I'm worried I'll do damage if I try to reverse what the mage did, so we may need to let it wear off naturally. She appears to be in no distress, and her vitals are all good.'

Merry reached out to Sadie with her mind, wincing at the ache that set up in her head. Still, she persevered.

Sadie, can you hear me?

For a long moment there was nothing, and then a faint sense of the little familiar blossomed in her head. Not words, but the impression the cat was not happy with the situation, along with a sense of urgency.

'Ah, I think she wants you to give it a try.'

Ellen cast a dubious glance at Merry over her shoulder. 'Are you sure?'

The ache in Merry's head intensified as she once again reached out to the cat and received the same sense of urgency in response. 'Yes. This is what Sadie wants.'

A tiny meow came from Sadie, her eyes blinking slowly as she fixed her gaze on Ellen.

'All right then, I'll give it a go.' Ellen closed her eyes, one hand on her heartstone and the other on Sadie's flank. Her lips moved in a spell too quiet for Merry to hear, but goose bumps swept over her to indicate magic was being employed.

After a long and tense moment, where she wondered if they had made the right call, Ellen opened her eyes and lifted her hand. Sadie's fur rippled and then she stood, her body trembling for a moment.

Her head swung round and she stared at Merry, eyes narrowed to slits. *I am going to tear that mage to shreds, and the idiot who carted me here and tossed me on the floor like a piece of garbage.*

Despite the ferocity in the familiar's words, and the way they made her head pound even more, Merry smiled. Sadie was going to be okay.

She reached out and patted the cat on the head, stroking the silky soft ears. 'I'm glad you're okay. It has been kind of lonely in my head.' The little cat nestled her head into Merry's hand, a soft purr rumbling in the silence.

Then the cat moved over to Ellen and smooched against her side. *Thank you.*

Ellen's smile was relieved as she reached out and ran her hand along the cat's sleek coat. 'You're welcome,' she said, not needing Merry to translate for her.

Now then, how do we get out of this hell hole? That enforcer is unhinged. We must not linger.

Merry grimaced at Sadie's description of Karl. It was true, he was not right in the head. If it hadn't been for

Kassandra intervening, who knew how far he would have gone. Speaking of Kassandra…

'Does anyone else think it was weird to have Kassandra defend me?'

'If what I heard about the oaths they are made to swear when they are initiated into the guild is true, she had no choice. Her brother was not wrong, he will not be able to trust her until that is broken,' said Ellen.

'What about him? He should have been bound by the same oath. Or do you think his was broken by a heart-stone, like Mage Fowler?' Even saying his name made the guilt and revulsion Merry felt at his manner of death rear up. Combined with the stench from the taint, it was all she could do not to throw up.

'It has to have been. But that doesn't explain why he was trained as an enforcer, when he clearly has Air magic. He's strong, too, strong enough to be a mage.'

At Ellen's words, Merry shivered. Her body still ached from the way he had lashed her with wind, and she had been unable to stir anything more than a mild breeze. Ellen had fixed her paralysis, but she was still blocked from accessing her magic. Yet Karl had no trouble wielding his, and neither did the Earth and Fire mages, and presumably the Spirit mage had no problem either. So why was Merry affected? She'd first thought it had been something the Earth mage had done to her, but thanks to Ellen's healing abilities the paralysis had gone, along with the worst of her aches, but not the block on her magic.

The poison is in the water, and you have shown consider-able ability with Water magic. Perhaps that is why you are having trouble.

Sadie's suggestion made as much sense as any. The sooner they found a way out of this room, and she got far enough away from the taint to test the theory out, the better. Merry got to her feet, still using the wall to aid her balance as she stumbled over to the door and tried the handle.

Locked, of course.

She turned to the others. 'Either of you know how to pick locks?'

Ellen shook her head, and Sadie's response was just as depressing. Merry faced the door again, wishing her head would stop aching so she could think. She stiff-ened, and then turned back to Ellen.

'You said that mage used nerve blockers to paralyse us. Could you do something similar in a magical sense?'

'I don't understand.' Ellen frowned at her, the flick-ering light from the lantern casting shadows on her face.

Merry explained Sadie's theory about the poisoned water affecting her magical ability. 'Could you block the taint from affecting me?'

'A nerve blocker wouldn't work, but I might be able to create a mental shield that will shut out the taint for a bit,' said Ellen, chewing at her bottom lip. 'But if I get it wrong, it could be dangerous.'

'More dangerous than sitting here and waiting for a

deranged enforcer with Air magic to do whatever it is he intends to do with us?'

At the grim reminder of what they faced, Ellen moved forward and placed a hand on the side of Merry's head. 'From what healers in the past generations have learned about where our magic comes from, witches and mages have an extra gland in their brain that gifts them with their abilities. We are taught to discern the gland and to differentiate between abilities when we do deep delving. This is normally only required when there is a brain injury of some sort, and the injured witch or mage is experiencing magical side effects.'

She clutched her heartstone with her free hand and gazed at Merry, a serious expression on her face. 'I have seen this done but never attempted it myself. For this to work, I need to isolate the area of the gland that deals with Water. It will show up as blue to my magic. Your other abilities, Earth and Air, will appear as green and white areas.'

That made sense, for Ellen to focus on colours within the gland. When Merry had used her Earth magic to spy out where everyone was when they'd been working to stop Lord Andel and his people mining heartstones, the Earth witches he had enslaved had pulsed with a green light in her mind, while the captured enforcers were red and the Spirit mage purple.

She gave a nod and indicated for Ellen to go ahead.

Ellen said, 'If this works, it will only be temporary.

Magic is resistant to tampering, so whatever you plan to do you need to do it fast.'

Seconds later warmth flared in Merry's head and for a blessed moment she felt normal again. No taint oozing through her brain and she could feel her connection to the heartstone that had been taken from her. It was somewhere above her. They would need to retrieve all their things before fleeing the dam, but first they had to get out of the room they were imprisoned in.

With Ellen still holding a hand to her head, Merry stretched out her own hand and placed it on the door beside the lock. She delved her senses into the metal, seeking the inner workings. It was a complicated jumble of pieces and she grimaced as she tried to figure out what part she needed to manipulate to unlock the door.

A hint of the taint leaked through the shield Ellen had created in her brain and Merry's heart rate spiked. She was running out of time. No seconds to waste on being precise. She clenched down on the lock, squeezing the parts into one lump, just as the block faded completely and she was left retching into the corner nearest the door at the return of the stench.

A soft click drifted through the air and she wiped her mouth and straightened up to see Ellen opening the door a crack. 'It worked.' Her friend wore a huge smile as she hurried over to Merry. 'How are you feeling?'

'Better now we can get out of here. Can you sense anyone out there?' As much as she wanted to get as far away from whatever was causing her taint as possible, she didn't want to risk running straight into some guards.

Ellen touched the wall beside the door. 'I can't detect anyone else on this level.'

'Good.' Merry pushed down her nausea and hurried over to the door, pushing it open fully and waving Sadie and Ellen ahead of her. Outside the room, she scanned the hall with even more pipes in the ceiling, though this section was high enough that they wouldn't bang their heads. Her heartstone had been to the left, while the sense of the taint was stronger to the right.

Again, Merry wanted to get as far away from it as possible, but this could be the only opportunity she had to find out what was making it. The stench was so strong, almost as strong as what she had felt when she had been near the rock pool.

Revulsion churned in her stomach as she lifted the lantern higher and headed to the right. Ellen and Sadie were at her back as she rounded a corner and found herself staring at a pulsing aqua coloured stone suspended in a clear vat of water, a pipe at the bottom leading to what appeared to be an outlet valve. The water around the stone was slimy with the taint, but the water below the valve was untainted.

The stone itself was about as big as Merry's fist and was the same blue green colour as the taint. It hurt Merry's eyes to look at it, and the urge to vomit so strong her stomach ached.

This was what was causing the taint. But it was

not yet spreading to the water below it. This stone was not what was poisoning the rock pool and leaching out to sea and into the underground water supply.

'There has to be another of these stones back at the rock pool,' she said in a low whisper to her friends.

'What is it?' Ellen asked.

Merry had worked with many precious gems while making jewellery to sell, and she was almost positive this was an aquamarine. A magically tainted aquamarine. But before she could tell her friend what she suspected a noise came from behind them.

They spun around, and Merry stiffened at the sight of Kassandra. The young woman's eyes were reddened, and her cheeks blotchy. But Merry pushed down her empathy. So what if the enforcer had been crying. She was the one who had chosen to go against the guild and help her insane brother.

Merry tensed, waiting for the outcry and for Kassandra to use her magic to immobilise them until reinforcements arrived.

But all the enforcer did was sling their packs off her shoulders and toss them on the floor between them. 'Here are your things. You need to leave. Before my brother and the others return.'

'You're helping us! Why?' Merry scurried forward and grabbed her pack, hands delving inside. Relief made her shake when she found the spell box and checked the charms she had gathered were still there. Her staff was also there and holding it in her hands helped to steady her.

'The guild should not force us to swear an oath to obey the rules of the guild master without question. I do believe that. But what Karl is proposing to do is wrong. No one deserves to be tortured.'

'He wants to torture me?' Merry's voice squeaked.

Kassandra's top lip curled up into one of disgust. 'He wants you to work for him. It's your friends he plans to torture, to make you do what he wants.'

Horror engulfed Merry at her words.

'There's no time to waste. You have to get out of here now.' Kassandra made a brusque shooing motion.

'How do I stop the poison?' Merry waved a hand at the stone behind her.

'You can't. Those stones were created by a powerful Water mage, and even he died in the making of the one that Karl placed in the rock pool at the Water focal point. Only a mage even more powerful than him would be able to destroy his creations, and they would most likely die in the attempt. Now, we need to stop wasting time. I've cleared the way to the back exit. Once I get you there, you're on your own.' She turned around and strode off without waiting to see if they were following.

Merry wasn't sure if they could trust her, but what choice did they have. After another look at the poisoned stone, she indicated for Ellen and Sadie to follow Kassandra, hoping they weren't making yet another mistake.

CHAPTER 10

Kassandra led them through a convoluted path of hallways, all with pipes snaking overhead. The farther they got from the poison stone, the better Merry felt. She could now reach out with her senses without suffering waves of nausea, though her head still ached. From the weary slump to Ellen's shoulders, her friend wasn't feeling much better. They'd had little rest and no water other than what Kassandra had given them on the forced march back to the dam.

Merry eyed the enforcer. 'Any chance of a drink and something to eat?'

Kassandra shot a glare her way. 'I had a hard enough time grabbing your belongings. Once you are on the other side of the dam, you will be able to drink the water and forage for food. You can't expect me to take care of everything.'

'We are grateful for your assistance, Kassandra,' said Ellen, saving Merry from biting back.

They hadn't forced Kassandra to help them. They had been doing a fine job of rescuing themselves when she showed up. Okay, it might not have been so easy for them to get their stuff, but they weren't useless.

'Just don't waste time. You need to get as far away from here as you can before Karl returns and finds out I helped you escape.'

Any ire Merry felt towards Kassandra fled at the thought of the enforcer having to face her insane brother's anger when he returned. 'We got out of that room by ourselves. Maybe he won't know you helped us.'

This time the look Kassandra gave Merry was incredulous. 'You expect him to believe you sneaked through a camp of armed militia and got your staff and packs, all without any of them noticing?'

'If you're so worried about what his reaction will be, why don't you come with us?'

Kassandra stopped walking and stared at Merry, a light of what appeared to be hope brimming in her eyes. Then she shook her head. 'I broke guild law when I helped my brother escape. I can't go back.' She shook her head. 'But you can give them a message for me.'

She sucked in a deep breath, and then words tumbled out in a rush, 'Tell Mage Fairweather there are traitors within the guild, working to undermine it. These traitors are recruiting mages and enforcers before they enter the tower for training. They have a way of falsifying the oath, so people like my brother are not bound to obey guild law and can hide the true nature of their abilities. I don't know who they are or how many of them are within the tower, but she needs to know she cannot trust her own people.'

Merry gaped at her. Traitors in the guild? 'These traitors, are they all working for Lord Andel?'

Kassandra shook her head. 'He's not the only lord who wants a return to a monarchy. Lord Andel is just the one who has gathered the most magical support, by forcing witches to swear oaths to obey him and subverting or forcing mages to do the same. If he isn't stopped, he will soon be too powerful for the guild or any of the other lords to go up against him.'

'Is he behind the smear campaign on the guild?' Ellen asked.

Kassandra gave a nod. 'It was his idea for those magic users who support the return of the monarchy to use unrest among the general citizens, and turn them against the guild, so that when he is ready to strike they will back him.' She scowled. 'It would not have come to this if the guild had not been so insular. Mage Fair-weather's iron control on when and how enforcers and mages were allowed to use their magic is what drove them to Andel's side and first turned the citizens against them.'

Having heard from Ellen how the witches and those without magic were being treated, Merry didn't blame the citizens for being angry with the guild. After her run in with Lord Andel, she was sure having him as king would be much worse. He had to be stopped. But going to the tower and giving Kassandra's message to Mage Fairweather would only result in her being ensnared by the guild, or worse.

'We can't go to the tower,' she said, 'but we will find a way to get your message to them.' Maybe she would be able to contact Gabriel. If there were traitors, he would be the only guild mage she was sure she could trust.

Kassandra frowned, but said nothing more as she set off again.

They soon reached a door that was barred and padlocked from the inside. Kassandra stepped to the side and said, 'I don't have the key and my brother will be able to tell if I use my ability to break the lock. It will be up to you to get this door open. I can help you no more.' With that she turned around and walked back the way they had come, taking the lantern with her.

Merry gripped her staff and willed it to glow, thankful for the lessening of the effects of the poison stone. Then she stretched out a hand and placed it on the padlock. As she had back at the tiny room she and the others had been locked in, but with far less effort and discomfort, she squeezed the padlock and it popped open.

She slid it off and then moved the bar to open the door, revelling in the sweet, fresh air that spilled through the opening. She ushered Sadie and Ellen ahead of her and then stepped through, closing the door behind her.

The sun was shining as they stepped out of the shadow of the dam wall. The grass was lush and green under Merry's feet and the stench of the taint faded with each step. If not for the exhaustion still dogging her, the growling of a stomach that had not been fed properly in days, and a throat that was so parched it hurt to swallow, she could almost enjoy the moment.

The track they were on was dirt and ran alongside a cliff that edged off a valley as lush as the grass. That would all be destroyed if the tainted water held at bay by the dam managed to spill over. Merry shuddered at the thought as they hurried away from the dam wall, eager to put as much distance between them and Karl's forces as possible. There were signs a number of people had passed this way recently, with the road churned up and the grass trampled. The sun was high overhead, serving to increase Merry's thirst, and her pace slowed despite her best intentions.

The valley widened after it curved around the cliff, taking them out of sight of anyone who might be patrolling on top of the dam wall, but they didn't stop to rest until they had travelled for over an hour and reached the edge of the forest she had seen the day before. They had no food or water, but Merry's legs were grateful for the reprieve as she sank onto the thick grass.

Sadie stood with her ears pricked as she looked back

the way they had come. *I do not believe we are being pursued. Perhaps our escape has not yet been noticed.*

Merry placed a hand on the ground beside her and closed her eyes as she sought to connect with the Earth, conscious of the heartstone in her bag thrumming through her senses. Her head ached with the effort, but she was able to briefly scan the land between them and the dam. Unlike when she had tried on the other side, she could sense small animals and insects living untainted lives, but nothing bigger to indicate a person and she hadn't seen any of the mages working for Lord Andel with a familiar.

'I can't sense anyone following us,' she said as she let go of her Earth magic and rubbed at her temples. 'But I don't think we should stay here too long.' Though her muscles protested at the mere thought of moving again, she knew it would be better to keep going for as long as they could. She got to her feet, head spinning with the movement, and then forced herself to start walking.

'It looks as if some of the people who lived on the other side of the dam managed to get across before the militia blocked the route,' said Ellen, pointing to what appeared to be the remnants of a camp beside the road as it snaked through the trees.

Though glad to know some people had made it, Merry could not forget the family who had died on the other side of the dam as they sought safety and had instead been poisoned. Kassandra had urged Merry and her friends to get word to the guild, but that would not get her any closer to finding a Water charm. Such a charm would be impossible to find until the taint had been cleared from the rock pool.

'We need to find a town, and someone who can send a message to Gabriel about what is going on here,' she said. He was a Water mage as well as an Air mage. Not that he would be able to destroy the poisoned stones on his own, if what Kassandra had said was true about the creation of them having taken the life of the most powerful Water mage in Tirana.

'He should know more Water mages he can trust to help him fix things.' She hoped.

Ellen peered through the trees. 'According to the map, there is a river in that direction,' she said, pointing off to the left. 'Most villages and towns are situated beside sources of fresh water. We should be able to find a courier or have them direct us to one.'

'Let's hope so.' Merry also hoped it wouldn't take them long to find a village or town. At this point, she'd be happy for a farm; somewhere they could beg for food and water. She didn't think Ellen was up to bartering her healing skills until she had fully recovered from their ordeal.

Merry's legs were aching, her muscles trembling, and that ever present headache wearing her down. She may have been able to open locks, but she didn't think any serious magic was possible in her weakened state. Their pace was far slower than normal as they trudged along the dirt road in search of the river Ellen's map had indicated.

Each step she took jarred Merry's body, and her head, but she forced herself to keep going. They were out of Karl's clutches, on the non-poisoned side of Marshland Province, and the tall trees lining the road provided relief from the sun. The shade felt heavenly, but it was the sight of dark blueish purple berries on a bush a few trees in that had her salivating.

'Please tell me these are edible,' she said, her voice cracking as she turned to Ellen.

Ellen's expression lit up. 'Blueberries.' She lunged forward and began picking the plump berries and shoving them in her mouth.

Merry quickly joined her, moaning in pleasure at the succulent sweetness as she bit into the first berry. Sadie also ate some of the berries, gaining much needed water even though the little cat complained about the taste. All too soon the bush was devoid of all berries and they set off again. Merry's fingers were stained purple and she was sure her mouth was the same. Not that it mattered what she looked like.

Her stomach still grumbled, not satisfied, but the juice of the berries had at least helped to soothe some of the dryness in her throat. They stopped late in the afternoon when they found a second blueberry bush, quickly stripping it of the sweet fruit. Her body screamed at her when they set off again, but she forced herself to keep placing one foot in front of the other. If she let herself falter, she didn't think she would have the energy or the will power to get moving again.

Shadows danced around them, dusk staining the sky a rich purple hue, when they finally reached the river. The water was fast moving, free of the taint, and Merry wanted to dive in. She stumbled forward, dropping her pack to the ground.

'Wait,' said Ellen, holding up a hand to stop Merry. 'I need to make sure the water is safe for us to drink. Just because it isn't tainted doesn't mean harmful bacteria may not be present.'

It took all of Merry's self-control to wait for Ellen to dip their wooden mugs into the river, sprinkle the water with her herbs, and murmur her spell.

Ellen handed one of the mugs to Merry. 'I added heartleaf to give us extra energy, but you need to sip slowly. Too much on an empty stomach could make you sick.'

Slowly!

Merry wanted to guzzle the water down, then throw herself into the river to fill her belly with as much of it as she could. Her hands shook with the effort to restrain her impulse as she followed Ellen's instructions.

Every tingly sip of water that slipped down her throat felt like nectar of the gods. No magical concoction could ever taste half as good. A soft meow came from near her feet, and Merry took a deep breath before placing the cup down on the ground for Sadie to drink out of.

As the tingle from Ellen's spell wove through Merry, her energy returned and some of her headache diminished. She was able to resist the urge to guzzle more water while helping Ellen refill their water skins. Her hands didn't even shake as the healer put herbs in each skin and completed her spell.

'That's the last of my herbs,' said Ellen. 'We will need to find a fresh water source or forage for more herbs, but this should at least keep us going for a while.'

With the berries long forgotten, Merry's stomach gave a loud grumble as they set off. The energy gifted by the magically enhanced water meant she was able to light her staff to ward off the deepening shadows. She was hopeful they would soon find their way to a village, or a bridge to cross over to the other side of the river. But night fell without any sign of either, and soon her head began to ache from willing the staff to remain lit. The glow it emitted pulsed in time with the pounding in her head, and one sharp pain had it go out completely.

'Merry, enough,' said Ellen as she placed a hand on Merry's arm. 'We're both exhausted and stumbling around in the dark is going to lead to one of us getting injured. We need to rest.'

Ellen is right. None of us is at our best. We can continue our search for a way across the river tomorrow.

If there even was a way across. Merry was starting to doubt they would ever make it to the other side of the river. It was as if all of Marshland was deserted. She was too exhausted to care about spending another night sleeping on the cold, hard ground. All she could hope was that the next day would see them finally get a break.

They set off again at dawn, sure the dirt road they followed would lead them to a bridge eventually. But when they did find a bridge, the goal to get to the other side of the river seemed even farther away, tears stinging Merry's eyes as she faced defeat.

The timber bridge had been demolished, only the pylons left standing at either end. Ellen placed a hand on jagged splinters sticking out of one of the pylons on their side of the river. 'It looks as though this was done recently.'

'Maybe they thought it would stop Karl and his goons getting across.' Whatever the reason, it was going to make it more difficult for Merry to find the help she needed to get rid of the taint at the Water focal point.

There's a boat in these bushes.

Boat turned out to be a dubious name for what Sadie had found. Merry parted the bushes and beheld a rickety contraption that looked likely to fall apart the minute it touched water. Yet it would have to do. The river was flowing too strongly and was too wide for them to be able to swim across in their weakened state. Besides, she might be able to use her Air magic and speed them across before it sank.

She hoped.

Merry's headache from the night before had diminished, even though her sleep had been less than restful, and she could sense the elemental power of the wind around her. She would just have to maintain her spell long enough to get them safely across to the other side.

She and Ellen tugged the boat out of the bushes and inspected their newest mode of transportation. Without the bushes to shield part of it, the boat looked in even worse shape and Merry feared what she was going to attempt was a fool's errand. Despite her misgivings, she helped Ellen tug it to the river's edge and then joined in the search for twigs and leaves to plug the worst of the holes.

With Ellen guiding her, Merry used Earth magic to strengthen the makeshift plugs, mentally willing them to be waterproof and not get washed away. Beside her, Ellen said the same litany out loud, and Merry could see and feel the twigs and leaves knitting together.

Maybe this crazy plan would work after all.

She and Ellen pushed the boat partially into the water, keeping a firm grip on the end to make sure it wasn't washed away in the current. The boat did not instantly fall apart, though it bucked in the current and Merry was worried it would be torn free. No water pooled in the bottom either, so their patches appeared to be holding. They piled their gear inside. Then Sadie hopped in.

Merry grounded herself with Earth as Ellen stepped into the boat, feeling the strain both physically and magically to hold it in place. Her arms were shaking when she was finally able to jump in and the boat slid fully off the bank and into the rushing current.

They were swept downstream immediately, passing the section of the damaged bridge on the other side within seconds. Merry took a deep breath, gripped her staff, and began a mental litany to will the wind to push the boat against the current, angling for the other side. For a long moment, nothing happened, and then the boat began to fight against the current, slowing moving towards the other bank.

Sweat broke out on Merry's face as she continued her silent spell. A cool sensation washed over her feet, but she ignored it, all her attention and energy focused on getting the rickety boat across the river.

Her concentration broke as Ellen gave a cry. 'We're sinking.'

Merry risked a downward glance and saw water pouring in through the holes in the boat, the makeshift patches tossing about in the water. Then she commanded the wind to blow harder, faster. They had to get across. Ellen's map said this river ended in a waterfall, much like the one at the rock pool. They did not want to be swept over the edge.

She was conscious of Ellen desperately working to bail out as much water as she could. It was a losing battle. There were too many holes. She had to stop the river water getting in the boat, but how?

She had used Water magic against the militia back at the cove when they were fleeing to *Hellcat*, pulling sea water and throwing it at them. Could she do the opposite here?

The sweat dripped down her face as she split her consciousness. Her staff grew hot enough to make her grit her teeth as she worked to force the water back through the holes and keep the wind blowing them across the river at the same time. Merry could feel the ache building behind her temples. She ignored the pain as best she could. They had to get across.

With one last ditch effort, she sent a gale of wind at the boat, making it shoot over the surface of the river and slam into the other bank with a jolt that splintered the rotting timber.

'Hurry,' she gasped out as her magic faded, head pounding so hard it was almost impossible to think. She tried to stand and failed.

She felt her arms being gripped, and she was dragged from the boat to land face down on the grassy bank. With a muffled groan, she rolled onto her side, summoning the energy to thank Ellen for the rescue.

But it wasn't Ellen leaning over her.

It was a stranger wearing a grey tunic, a cresting wave embroidered in blue on the left of his chest.

Voices sounded nearby, and Merry craned her neck to see more men and women in similar attire. Ellen was standing, with her arms twisted behind her back and a pained expression on her face, while Sadie was nowhere to be seen.

Hands grasped Merry's arms and she was roughly pulled to her feet. Her knees would not support her weight, and she fell. With a mumbled curse, the man who had pulled her up slung her over his shoulder. Then a command was given, and he set off.

Merry hung down, exhausted and in too much pain to even contemplate escape. She could only hope that these were the good guys. After all, they were on the untainted side of the province and she had never seen that type of militia uniform before.

After checking to see that more of the militia carried their gear, including her staff, Merry lowered her head and let her body go limp. As undignified as the means of transportation was, she didn't have the energy to walk. She barely had the energy to stay awake, though she wished for oblivion as that might help with her aching head.

Ellen trudged along behind her, a woman keeping a firm grip on her shoulder, the healer's requests to heal Merry ignored. Ordered to remain silent, Merry's friend cast concerned glances her way, and she tried to look more lively. She would be fine, once she had some rest, and she didn't want her friend to worry unnecessarily.

After a short time, Merry was tossed down in the back of a carriage, and Ellen settled in beside her. Familiar warmth flooded through Merry as her friend did what she could to ease the effects of magical exhaustion without access to her herbs. She kept apologising in a low voice, but Merry told her it was okay.

There was no sign of Sadie, and Merry's brain was in too much of a fog for her to reach out to the familiar.

She could only hope the black cat found a way to follow them.

She must have dozed off at some stage because the sun was low in the sky, signalling the end of day, when the carriage came to a stop and the door was opened. Her legs still shook, but she could stand upright on her own once she was on the ground, thanks to her rest and the healing from Ellen.

In front of her was a manor house that bore a strong resemblance to the one Lord Andel called home. As they were marched towards it, Merry could only hope they weren't about to be thrown into yet another dungeon.

CHAPTER 11

They were marched to the front door, which was open, and stepped into a wide foyer with a patterned tile floor in varying shades of blue. The effect was distracting, like walking across water. After her fight with the river, Merry had had enough of water for a while.

The militia made them stand in the centre of the foyer, facing a set of timber stairs that led to a balcony that ran around the sides of the top floor. A young woman in a flowing blue dress was standing at the top of the stairs, blonde hair braided in a coil on the top of her head. A gold coronet was nestled atop her hair, gleaming in the light of the torches lining the foyer walls as she gracefully descended the stairs.

She kept walking, one beringed hand holding up the hem of her long dress, until she stood directly in front of Merry and Ellen, her clear blue eyes cold. 'How dare you show your face in my province, after what you have wrought with your evil magic.'

Merry gave a start, sharing a puzzled glance with Ellen before stammering out a response. 'All I did was push the boat across the river. I didn't mean for it to break. Though, to be fair, it was in a bad way before I got to it.'

The woman's brow creased. 'What are you talking about?'

'Using Air magic to speed the boat across the river before it sank.' Merry wondered if she should also mention how she had used Water magic to get rid of the water that had already filled the boat. From her dress, this woman was a Water witch. She might know of a Water mage powerful enough to destroy the poisoned aquamarine in the dam, and in the waterfall.

'I don't care what you did to a stupid old boat. I'm talking about how you and the other renegades have poisoned half my land.' Her eyes narrowed as she scanned them. Then she looked to the man who had led them inside. 'Did you search them for poison?'

'We did, Lady Beatrice. All we found were some herbal potions and this.' He produced Merry's spell box and handed it to the woman.

She opened it up and peered inside, eyes going wide as she plucked out Merry's heartstone.

Merry felt a wrench on her connection with the heartstone and glared at Lady Beatrice as a flash of heat flared in her solar plexus. The other woman gave a gasp, dropped the stone back into the spell box and snapped the lid shut. Then she rubbed her fingertips on her dress and gazed haughtily at Merry.

'What sabotage were you planning to do in my province?'

'We're not here to sabotage anything. We just need to find a Water mage.'

'Why? So you can poison this half of the province as well?' She gave an angry shake of her head, almost dislodging her coronet. 'I told the last messenger that I will not bow to ultimatums. Marshland will never join the renegade faction and support the return of a monarchy.'

Merry's eyes widened. 'We're not with them. We want to stop them.' Well, stop the poisoning. Merry had no intention in getting embroiled in the looming battle between those who supported Lord Andel's bid for the throne and the guild. She planned to be long gone before the situation in Tirana got any worse. But to get home, she needed the poisoned aquamarine gone from the Water focal point.

Lady Beatrice gave a most unladylike snort. 'Of course you are with them. My guards tracked you from the moment you left the dam.'

'We didn't leave. We escaped.' Merry thought better of mentioning Kassandra's involvement in that escape. 'We arrived a couple days ago, only to realise after our ship had left that all the water was poisoned. We ran out of supplies and were trying to get past the dam wall, to this side, when we were captured and imprisoned by the renegades.'

'You expect me to believe that?'

Merry was suddenly so tired it was hard to keep standing. She held back a yawn, eyes watering, and said, 'You can believe what you want. I'm telling the truth. We need to find as many Water mages as we can to fix the taint, so if you have any of them around that would be fantastic. If not, we need to send word to the guild tower. But the only mage you should be trusting from the guild right now is Gabriel Fairweather.'

'Gabriel Fairweather?'

It was an effort for Merry to keep her eyes open, but she hadn't missed the startled expression that crossed Lady Beatrice's face at the mention of Gabriel. Before she could say anything more, her knees once again gave out on her, only the quick reflexes of the militia guard beside her stopping her from slamming into the tiled floor.

'Merry needs healing,' said Ellen, her tone affronted. 'She is magically exhausted from helping us escape. She hasn't eaten for days and is severely dehydrated. The rest of your questions will have to wait.'

Lady Beatrice gave a flurry of orders, and the guard holding Merry up scooped her into his arms. He strode down a hall that led alongside the left of the staircase and soon she was placed on a low couch while Ellen kneeled at her side. The expected flood of warmth that came was less than usual, and as soon as she was strong enough Merry sat up and pushed her friend away. She looked to where Lady Beatrice stood with her arms crossed in front of her chest on the other side of the room.

'Ellen is just as exhausted, starved and dehydrated as me. She should be resting, not trying to heal anyone.'

Lady Beatrice summoned a grey garbed servant. 'Janelle, please ask Master Nelson to join us, and then head to the kitchens and request suitable refreshments be prepared for our… guests.'

Merry slumped back on the couch, urging Ellen to join her as they waited for this Master Nelson to appear. Lady Beatrice remained where she stood, only raising one eyebrow when Sadie sauntered into the room and jumped up onto Merry's lap.

Merry lifted a hand that felt ten times heavier than it should to stroke the cat's sleek black fur. *I was starting to think you'd been left behind at the river.*

Sadie nudged her hand. *I thought it best to keep my presence hidden until I could ascertain if these people were friend or foe, in case I needed to mount a rescue.*

Merry let her hand fall to the side as a man with bushy brown hair bustled in, his green tunic rumpled and marked with stains. Despite his appearance, his voice was firm as he barked orders. Soon he sat in a chair beside the couch and was rummaging through a pouch similar to the one Ellen used to carry her herbal remedies.

As he laid a hand on Merry's forehead and warmth

flooded through her, she let herself relax and waited for the healing to work. Once she was able to stand up without collapsing, she would tackle the problem of how to remove the poisonous stone from the Water focal point.

By the time Master Nelson had finished healing Merry and had moved on to Ellen, the servant had returned with a large platter with a number of covered plates on top of it. A second servant came behind her with a tray of drinks. Lady Beatrice had taken a seat at some stage through Merry's healing and was now perched on the edge of a couch opposite her. The servants attended to the lady of the manor first, while Merry had to wait until Master Nelson had healed Ellen and then perused the refreshments to determine what was appropriate for them to eat after being so long without proper food or water.

When he handed Merry a bowl of soup, she cast an envious glance at the sugar crusted pastry Lady Beatrice was nibbling on. Still, soup was better than nothing. She took her first spoonful, conscious of the healer's admonition to go slow. It was hard to restrain her impulse to gulp it down. The soup was delicious, full of flavour, and her stomach grumbled at the first taste, demanding more. Yet she paced herself and continued to slowly spoon in mouthfuls until the bowl was empty.

Sadie was not forgotten either, bowls of water and minced up fish in gravy on a silver tray set on the floor at Merry's feet. After finishing her meal, the little cat sat beside Merry and set about washing and grooming herself until her coat was once again sleek and glossy.

'We will let that settle, and soon you will be able to eat more solid food,' said Master Nelson, standing beside the couch and giving a satisfied nod. 'The three of you will need to rest for a couple of days, to fully regain your strength, but will all make a full recovery.' He peered over at Merry. 'But you, young lady, are not to use your magic for at least a week. Magical exhaustion is not something to trifle with. You risk burn out by pushing yourself too far, and worse.'

Merry didn't want to know what that worse could be, but he told her with relish about mages who had overextended themselves and fallen into comas, some of them to never wake, their bodies wasting away.

The way everything was going, not using magic for a week was going to be a challenge, but she would do her best. Funny to think she had lived nineteen years never knowing she was capable of magic, and now the thought of not using it for a week left a strange feeling. With the need to remove the taint so she could get her Water charm, magic would have to be involved. She hoped the guild would be able to take care of that.

She looked over to Lady Beatrice. Before she could speak, the ruler of Marshland Province ushered Nelson and the servants out, though four of the militiamen remained in the room, including the one who appeared to be in charge.

'You say you are not part of the group who hold my

province hostage,' said Lady Beatrice, pinning a cold stare on Merry. 'Who are you?'

'We're just people who wound up in the wrong place at the wrong time,' said Merry, her words summing up her entire time in Tirana. 'We were travelling to the Water focal point, for personal reasons, when we got caught up in all this mess.'

'Why were you seeking the rock pool?'

'As I said, it's personal.'

'I don't care how personal it is. I need to determine how much of a threat you pose to my province and my people. You will tell me why you seek the rock pool.' Lady Beatrice lifted her chin and eyed Merry, clearly expecting an immediate response.

Considering what was going on at the dam, she didn't blame Lady Beatrice for being suspicious. 'I need a strong Water charm for a spell. The only place I can get it is from the rock pool.'

Lady Beatrice narrowed her eyes, and then gave a toss of her head. 'There will be no charms until that traitorous enforcer who threatened to poison my entire province is dealt with, and the taint he unleashed removed.'

'It's a poison stone,' said Merry, seeing no reason not to tell the truth. 'An aquamarine. A powerful Water mage created two of them. One is sitting inside the dam and the other, a larger one, is in the rock pool.' She filled Lady Beatrice in on what Kassandra had told them, and what they had discovered for themselves, including

Lord Andel's plan to return the rule of Tirana to a monarchy.

'Lord Andel's involvement comes as no surprise, though I had not realised he had so much support. As for this enforcer you say helped you, do you trust her? This Kassandra?'

Merry shook her head. 'I do believe her about the Water mage and there being traitors in the guild. That's why I said you need to contact Gabriel Fairweather. He's the only one we can be sure is not involved in Lord Andel's plot.'

Sorrow wreathed Lady Beatrice's brow. 'When people beyond the dam wall first sickened, and we realised the water was the cause, some of the best Water witches in the province attempted to find the source to cure it. They died horrible deaths, along with all those who had come into contact with the poisoned water. I immediately sent word to the guild, and my scouts advise me a delegation will be here within the hour. We can only hope this group does not include any of these traitors.'

She stood and began to pace. 'Shortly before the poison first appeared in the water, I received a courier with a message from Lord Andel. In it he proclaimed his intention to push for a return to a monarchy, with the guild and all magic users subject to the will of the king, and himself as the head of state. He wished to know whether Marshland would support him in his endeavour. Given that my family has a long tradition of producing those strong in Water magic, I questioned his reasoning in approaching me.'

She wore a wry smile as she waved a hand over her blue dress. 'I am by no means as powerful as my great-grandfather was, the mage who built the dam and increased the profitable land in our province threefold, but I do possess significant ability with Water magic. To agree to Lord Andel's proposal would make me subject to his will. But even if I had no elemental ability, I would have said no. King Reagan was prejudiced in his dealings with those of the nobility who possessed magic, and I would never willingly return to a state of rule where that may once again come to pass.'

Now her expression was grim. 'The poison appeared a week after I gave them my answer. When it became clear we could not cure it, I ordered a retreat to this side of the dam wall. Many people made it across, and then word came that an enemy force had taken up residence in the dam itself, cutting off the retreat for those still on the other side. Furthermore, I received an ultimatum. Either I threw my support in behind Lord Andel, or they would destroy the dam and flood the valley with tainted water, turning prime grazing land back into the marsh it once was and poisoning the waterways.'

It was a sobering thought.

Lady Beatrice looked as if she had more to say, but a knock at the door interrupted her. At her command, a servant entered and gave a low bow. 'The delegation from the guild have arrived, Lady Beatrice.'

'Thank you. You may show them in.'

Janelle disappeared, leaving the door open, and shortly reappeared to usher a number of Water mages and one cat into the parlour. A happy feeling bubbled up inside Merry at the sight of Gabriel Fairweather and his familiar, Beethoven. Some of her joy faded when she spotted the enforcer who had tried to kidnap her back on *Hellcat*, and five of his cronies, behind the mages. How in hell had they ended up here, when they'd been dropped off in a cove days ago?

Gabriel's gaze was fixed on Lady Beatrice, and before Merry could wave to get his attention, the other woman surged forward and blocked her view.

'Gabriel,' said Lady Beatrice, her voice lilting as she extended a hand towards him. 'How good it is to see you again. Though I wish it were under better circumstances.' She indicated for him to sit on the couch and then perched close beside him, her upper body leaning towards his.

Gabriel murmured a greeting as he scanned the room. His eyes widened when his gaze met Merry's. He shot to his feet and crossed the room in quick strides to stand in front of her.

'Merry, it is good to see you are well, and were not caught up in the earthquake that hit Taranganberg Province shortly after we parted company.' He ducked his head and nodded at Ellen. 'You also, Miss Hayland.'

'You know each other.' Lady Beatrice's tone was flat.

Gabriel flushed and turned back to face her. 'Miss

Meadows, and Miss Hayland of course, assisted the guild with some troubles in Taranganberg. There was an earthquake shortly after we parted company, and naturally I was concerned about their wellbeing.'

Troubles. Such an innocuous term for stopping Lord Andel from getting his hands on more heartstones to use to enslave witches and mages. As for the earthquake, Merry wondered if Gabriel knew she was the cause of it.

He suspected.

The voice in Merry's head was deeper than Sadie's. She scanned the room to find Gabriel's grey and white familiar perched on the arm of the couch where Lady Beatrice was once again ushering the mage to sit.

Merry scanned the faces of the other six mages who had come with Gabriel. All of them wore blue robes. Water mages. But there was no telling if any of them was a traitor. She looked over at Beethoven and telepathically informed him what they had been told by Kassandra.

The cat's green eyes widened. *I will inform Gabriel.*

Merry, watching as Lady Beatrice began filling Gabriel in about the troubles her province was facing, could tell the moment the message had been passed along. Gabriel stiffened, his gaze shooting to Merry for a brief moment, before he glanced over at the mages who had accompanied him. But he gave no other indication that anything was amiss.

He turned his full attention back to Lady Beatrice, who detailed the ultimatum she had received. She finished by adding the information given to her by Merry and Ellen.

He turned back to Merry once she was done. 'I wish we could have done more, to prevent Karl escaping and causing you harm.' He stood up and came over to kneel beside her, reaching out to take her hand. 'You should never have had to suffer through what you did. The guild owes you a debt of gratitude for your help, both with the wind golem and with stopping the illegal mining of heartstones. This was poor repayment.'

His grey eyes were sincere as he gazed at her, and the warmth of his hand on hers sent a thrill through her body. Merry flushed and looked over his shoulder, spotting a sour expression on Lady Beatrice's face as she watched them. Adrian, who had moved to take a seat beside Ellen, looked equally as sour.

She cleared her throat as she pulled her hand free and managed a smile for Gabriel. 'I think it's clear Karl hasn't been a true member of the guild for some time.' He and many others, if what Kassandra had said was true, though she wasn't going to mention that with six mages she did not know in the room.

Neither Lady Beatrice nor Gabriel brought the matter up either.

Merry scanned the enforcers lined up against the wall near the doorway, aware Karl might not be the only traitorous enforcer in the guild.

She looked over to Adrian. 'I thought you lot were making your way to the guild tower, to report on what is happening at Greystone?' He had always seemed zealous in following guild law, but appearances could be deceptive.

Adrian shot her a cool look. 'I don't discuss guild affairs with criminals.'

'Enough, Adrian,' said Gabriel, his tone sharp as he stood. 'Merry is far from a criminal. I expect you to treat her with respect.'

Adrian flushed as he inclined his head. 'Your pardon.'

It didn't escape Merry's attention that the words were grudgingly said.

'We encountered Adrian and his squad on the road between here and Marshland,' said Gabriel. 'He informed me half his team were on their way to the tower with news of the events in Greystone, while he and the others were continuing on to Marshland in search of a fugitive witch.' A wry grin curved his lips. 'He failed to mention which witch he was after.'

Lady Beatrice delicately cleared her throat as she glided forward and tapped Gabriel on the arm. 'I am sure you are famished after your long journey. We can continue this conversation over dinner.'

With a loud clap, she summoned Janelle and issued orders for rooms to be made up to house the guild dele-gation. She paused and looked at Merry, the sour expression from before making a brief return as she said, 'A room for these two as well.' Then she led them into a large dining room, where Gabriel was seated on

Lady Beatrice's right, and one of the other mages on her left.

The rest of the mages were shown to the closest seats, while Merry and Ellen were shunted down to the end of the table. Adrian was seated next to Ellen, but other than a dark stare Merry's way when he first sat down, he seemed more interested in talking to her friend. The enforcer beside Merry didn't seem inclined to talk to anyone, so that left Merry to watch the rest of the people at the table.

Like the enforcer beside her, the mages that had arrived with Gabriel were quiet, as were the remaining enforcers. The only person who seemed inclined to chat was Lady Beatrice and she kept her focus on Gabriel, the attention she lavished on him making it clear she considered him the only person at the table worth her interest. For his part, he remained unfailingly polite and made several attempts to include the mages sitting near him in the conversation. Lady Beatrice would quickly head off the attempt, placing a hand on Gabriel's arm to regain his full attention.

Seeing her monopolising his time, and the way she leaned in so close and acted as if they were the only two in the room, made Merry cringe. It was clear Gabriel was not as enamoured with the young ruler of Marsh-land Province as Lady Beatrice was with him. He'd been far more engaged during his interactions with Merry, even the ones when he had tried to arrest her. In the cave, when they'd been hiding from Lord Andel's men, there had been no distance between them at all.

As she remembered the feel of his hard body pressed up against hers, Gabriel looked down the table towards her and she flushed, pleased he wouldn't be able to tell what she was thinking. Still, the heat in her cheeks made her glad when Janelle and a host of other servants entered the dining room, carrying trays of delicious smelling food, and blocked her view of Gabriel for a moment.

Lady Beatrice flirted her way through the late meal. Merry and Ellen were offered simple fare, on Master Nelson's orders. They were also given water to drink in plain tumblers, while the rest were served a ruby coloured wine in fancy glasses. Not that Merry cared. She was just happy to fill her belly for the first time in days, and to be able to drink as much water as she liked.

The healing she had received had made her feel ten times better, but Master Nelson had not been wrong in saying it would take time for her body to heal properly. She was glad when the meal was over, and she and Ellen were ushered off to a room with twin beds.

There was no time to talk to Gabriel, as he was still being monopolised by Lady Beatrice, but he sent a message to Merry via Beethoven as she walked out of the dining room.

Gabriel wishes me to tell you he is pleased to see you again and hopes to talk to you further once the matter with the poisoned water is taken care of. A dry tone accompanied his next words. *What he didn't say, but I have no doubt he thinks, is that he would much rather be talking to you than Lady Beatrice. She was rather forthright about her intentions towards him on the last occasion they met. But you may rest assured that he finds the company of runaway witches far more interesting, even if they have been in the habit of hitting him over the head.*

Merry smiled at that last bit, glowing internally at the idea Gabriel would rather be spending time with her than Lady Beatrice. *I promised not to hit him again as long as he didn't try to arrest me.*

Then he should be safe. Despite his aunt's demands, Gabriel has no intention of forcing you to attend the tower against your will. He wishes you a good night and looks forward to learning more about what we will face at the dam directly from you in the morning.

Merry broadcast a mental goodnight to Beethoven and went to sleep with a smile, looking forward to what the next day would hold, even if it meant going up against Karl and his group and rooting out possible traitors among the mages who had accompanied Gabriel.

CHAPTER 12

$\mathcal{M}$erry blinked up at the high ceiling above her, her gaze tracing the thick wood beams that criss-crossed the room, and for a moment she was not sure where she was. Then memory returned and she knew she was in the bedroom she was sharing with Ellen and Sadie in the manor house in Marshland Province. It had been so long since she had slept in a real bed, she had tumbled into it after making good use of the spacious bathroom in the guest wing, finally getting to wash out the remnants of the homemade dye Ellen had concocted to disguise her purple hair.

Going to sleep clean and fed, and in a comfortable bed with soft linen, wearing a plain calico nightgown supplied by Lady Beatrice's servant, Janelle, had felt luxurious after far too many nights spent sleeping on the ground with no blankets let alone a pillow. She'd sunk onto the mattress and drifted off as soon as her head hit the pillow, until someone had called her name and woken her.

At least, she thought she'd heard someone call out to her.

The soft light of the moon, glinting through the window between the twin beds, cast shadows over the room's solid timber furnishings. She could hear Ellen's quiet breathing but there was no other sound, no sign of whoever had woken her.

Merry moved her feet, seeking the warm lump that Sadie made when she curled up on the end of the bed, but the little black cat was not there. She sat up, squinting at the light coming around the edge of the bedroom door. It was slightly ajar, though she distinctly remembered Ellen closing it after she had used the bathroom.

Had Sadie gone out? How would she have opened the door?

Merry telepathically reached out to the familiar. *Sadie, is everything okay?*

A soft scrape came from within the room, near the large wardrobe on the opposite wall, and Merry turned to face it.

Merry! Intruders!

Merry gasped and threw aside the bedding, lurching to her feet as a dark shape lunged out of the shadows beside the wardrobe and barrelled towards her. The light from the doorway glinted off a drawn sword. A scream caught in her throat, Merry grabbed her blanket and flung it at the intruder, tangling it around the end of the sword. Shouts rang out in the hallway and the clashing of swords came nearby, accompanied by cursing.

Ellen lunged out of bed and latched on to the intruder's back. Goose bumps swept over Merry as the healer worked her magic. The swordsman was in the process of untangling his sword, but now he fell to the ground, unconscious.

Merry hadn't even thought of using magic to ward off the attack and was thankful for her friend's quick thinking. She got off the bed and scooped up her staff before running to the door and wrenching it open fully. Then she froze for a moment at the sight of Gabriel in a pale blue nightshirt that left his muscular calves and bare feet visible. He stood in the middle of the hall, back to back with Adrian, who was also in a nightshirt and barefooted.

Gabriel was wielding his Air magic against men wearing Lord Andel's militia, using it to push them back down the hall, while Adrian was using his telekinesis to the same effect. As the intruders fought to get past the two men, a horn blew in the distance. Then a blinding flash of light came, accompanied by acrid smoke that filled the hall. It set Merry coughing and her eyes stung. She covered her mouth and nose, but it didn't help. She coughed even more, panicking when she felt her throat closing over.

Ellen pulled her back into the room and slammed the door shut.

The healer placed a hand on Merry's throat and soothing warmth flared at her touch. Almost immediately the choking and coughing eased. Merry's throat still felt dry and abraded, and her chest was sore from coughing but at least she could breathe. But what about Gabriel? He had been in the hallway, directly in the smoke.

She went back to the door, willing a wall of wind to wrap itself around her to protect her from the smoke, and wrenched it open. Adrian was on the ground, his body spasming from violent coughing, while Gabriel stood beside him, wind whipping the hem of his night-shirt as he wound the smoke into a funnel. He gazed over at her; his grey eyes solemn as he gave a nod. Then he strode into her room, still focusing on the smoke funnel as he walked over to the window.

As Ellen ran outside to take care of the downed enforcer, Merry wrenched open the window and Gabriel sent the smoke funnel outside and off into the distance. Goose bumps rippled over her skin, far more than whenever Ellen used healing magic. Gabriel flicked both hands outward, his lips chanting a silent spell as the funnel of smoke lost its shape and dispersed harmlessly through the air.

'That should alleviate the effects,' said Gabriel as he closed the window and then turned to face Merry. 'Are you all right?' His face was wreathed in shadows but there was no mistaking the concern in his eyes as he leaned closer.

Merry rubbed her throat. 'I'm fine now. Thanks to Ellen. How about you?'

'I was able to block the gas from entering my lungs, but Adrian was not so lucky.' Grim faced, Gabriel strode back to the hall to where Ellen was treating Adrian.

The enforcer was pale as he got to his feet and bowed to Ellen. 'Thank you for the healing, Miss Hayland. I am in your debt.' His voice was scratchy, but he appeared to be recovering from whatever was in the smoke.

Ellen blushed and gave a quick nod. 'There is no debt.' Then she turned away. 'I must see if anyone else needs healing.'

Adrian stared after her as she hurried off down the hall, his expression far softer than whenever he was interacting with Merry. But then, he had never tried to arrest Ellen.

Gabriel clapped Adrian on the shoulder. 'I can no longer hear fighting, but we must make sure it is safe for Miss Hayland as she renders her healing.'

The softness left Adrian's face and he gave a sharp nod. 'I will protect Miss Hayland.' He strode off down the hall after her without waiting for a response, night-shirt slapping around his calves, picking up speed as he went.

Merry hurried after him. Gabriel was right. The clashing of swords had stopped, though there was still plenty of shouting going on. He was also right about them needing to keep an eye on Ellen. While she had proved over and over again how resourceful and quick-witted she was, she would be vulnerable if she were immersed in healing.

Gabriel strode along at Merry's side, and they wound their way through the house, using the raised voices to guide them. He didn't appear discomfited to be attired in his nightshirt, so she figured it was okay for her to be in a similar state, though the tiles were cool beneath her bare feet. They found the cause of the commotion in the large foyer.

Lady Beatrice stood amidst a cluster of her militia, wearing a shimmering blue robe over a nightgown of the same design. Her long blonde hair flowed down her back in a sleek wave as she issued orders. Merry reached up and touched the tangled mess of hair on her own head, wincing at the sight she must make. But it couldn't be helped, and how she looked was the least of her concerns.

Master Nelson was in the foyer as well, treating a number of people who were coughing and looked to be having trouble breathing, though none of them appeared to be as bad as Adrian had been. Ellen joined Master Nelson and soon the coughing and gasping sounds lessened.

Lady Beatrice finished conferring with the head of her militia and then glided across the tiled floor, her beaded blue slippers making no sound as she headed for

Gabriel. There was no sign in her immaculate grooming that she had been rudely awoken in the middle of the night.

'I fear our hospitality has not been up to our usual standard.' Lady Beatrice inclined her head as she placed a hand on Gabriel's arm, a rueful smile on her face.

'It is not your fault. They were clearly after Merry.' Gabriel turned and faced Merry, dislodging Lady Beatrice's hand in the process.

'Me?' Merry's heart thudded as Gabriel moved closer, with a look of concern.

'From what we observed, this lot were a distraction. Meant to send us into disarray while the man Miss Hayland subdued went after you. I feared something like this might happen, that you would be a target, and had Beethoven watching over your room. He alerted me to the intruder. I am just sorry I did not get to your room faster.' His expression was chagrined. 'I would not forgive myself if any harm came to you. Beethoven said he had sent you a warning, so you were not caught unawares.'

That explained what had woken her. It must have been Beethoven calling out to her telepathically. But why hadn't he explained more? She scanned the room, not seeing the grey and white cat or Sadie. In fact, other than Sadie calling out that there were intruders, she had not heard from her since the initial attack.

'Where are Sadie and Beethoven?'

Here.

Sadie's mental voice was soft as a sigh and Merry turned to see her entering the room side by side with Beethoven. They shuffled along slowly, both with glassy eyes. *That gas you were hit with was not the only one the intruders had. I don't believe I have ever felt so tired as I do now.* Sadie stopped moving, body trembling.

Merry scooped Sadie into her arms, the little cat's body going limp. Fear thickening her throat, she ran across the room to where Ellen and Master Nelson were treating the gassed militia, Gabriel at her side with an equally limp Beethoven in his arms.

'Sadie and Beethoven have been drugged,' Merry said as she kneeled down beside Ellen, careful not to jostle the familiar in her haste.

Ellen quickly twisted around and placed a hand on Sadie's head. Goose bumps rose on Merry's arms, even as her heart thudded loud in her ears. Sadie had to be okay. She could not lose her.

After a moment, Ellen said, 'It's a sedative. I'll speed it through her system, and she should be fine.'

Relief threatened to make Merry as limp as Sadie. She took steadying breaths as Ellen worked her magic. Within moments both familiars were looking more alert.

Merry got to her feet once Sadie had jumped out of her arms. Gabriel was still at her side, and she was again conscious of how dishevelled she must look, having gone to bed with wet hair. She flushed, finger combing her hair as Lady Beatrice glided over to them.

'Why do you believe Merry was the target?' From the tone of her voice, and the dismissive glance she gave Merry, Lady Beatrice couldn't understand why anyone would go to so much effort on her behalf.

'Merry has proved extremely resourceful, when faced with seemingly insurmountable obstacles, and her magical ability is substantial. She has already ruined one of Lord Andel's schemes. He would not want her interfering further. This means we need to do everything we can to keep her safe.' Gabriel's voice rang with fervour, and the gaze he cast at Merry was just as intense.

Merry caught a look of speculation on Lady Beatrice's face and ducked her head, aware her cheeks were flushing. Gabriel had moved even closer to her, warmth spreading through her body at his nearness. His hand came up to cup Merry's chin, lifting her head, his grey eyes sincere.

'I won't let them hurt you, Merry. I promise.'

Caught in his gaze, conscious of Lady Beatrice watching on, Merry didn't know what to say.

She was spared from responding when the head of the Marshland militia strode over to Lady Beatrice's side. 'My lady, my men went to retrieve the man Miss Hayland said she rendered unconscious, but he was gone.'

Ellen hurried over to join them. 'He should still be sleeping, unless he had a healer to tend to him,' she said.

'He must have had help,' said Lady Beatrice, lips pursed as she scanned the collection of people in the foyer. 'He would also have required help to get inside the manor, and to find Merry's room.'

She pinned her gaze on Gabriel, for once without the coyness. 'You have a guild traitor within your party.'

Gabriel didn't flinch. 'It appears so.'

She turned away, snapping out orders to her militia commander. Soon a search had been conducted, and Lady Beatrice's expression was sour to learn that not only was one guild mage missing, but also three members of her own household.

'I found this in Wesley's room,' said one of the militia guards as she held up a vial. 'Master Nelson tells me it contains traces of the sedative that was used to incapacitate Mage Fairweather's familiar and the other cat. Many of Wesley's belongings are gone, as are those of his son and daughter-in-law.'

'So, the guild aren't the only ones with traitors in their midst,' said Merry, earning a dark glare from Lady Beatrice. She ignored the other woman and turned back to Gabriel.

'They could have fled to the dam, to tell Karl what we have planned.' Not that they had planned much, other than to head to the dam in the morning, and to chase Karl and his goons off so they could try to remove the taint from the poison stone inside the dam.

'It nears dawn,' said Lady Beatrice. 'Since the night is lost to us, along with the element of surprise, I propose we dress and head straight to the dam. There is no telling what mischief this guild traitor of yours will do now that the attempt on Merry's life has failed.' From her tone, she still couldn't see why anyone considered Merry such a threat that they would attack her when she was surrounded by allies.

Merry wasn't sure why she had been the target either. If Gabriel was even right about that. Yes, she had ruined Lord Andel's plan at the heartstone mine, and escaped from Karl, but surely Gabriel and the threat of the guild would be more worrisome. There was no time to worry about that now. She and Ellen headed back to their room to get changed into their cleaned dresses.

Janelle appeared with a simple breakfast and a mug of hot chicory laced coffee for them both, which helped to ward off the chill in the night air. She could see outside the window that the sky was lightening.

By the time she was back downstairs, her pack on her back and staff in hand, dawn had arrived.

Gabriel, once again wearing his blue and white mage robe over a white shirt and black trousers, strode to her side with a concerned expression. 'Master Nelson tells me you are not to use magic for a week. Perhaps it would be best if you were to remain here. We do not want you to risk magically exhausting yourself.'

Merry shook her head. 'I have to come. I have to get to the focal point to get a charm.' She couldn't remember if she'd told him about the transportation spell and was loath to do so now with so many people crowded around them. 'But I won't do magic. That is what you and the other Water mages are here for.'

They were one Water mage down, with the woman who had accompanied Gabriel to Marshland having disappeared, but Lady Beatrice had called in every Water witch she could find. As they headed outside and loaded into horse drawn carriages, Merry just hoped they would be enough, and that she would be able to keep her promise to not use any magic. She didn't want to risk full magical exhaustion and any of the consequences Master Nelson had listed. But they had no idea what they would encounter when they reached the dam. All she knew for sure was that Karl and the others were bound to put up a fight.

Gabriel sat beside her in the carriage. Lady Beatrice on the seat opposite watching them with narrowed eyes. Ellen, Adrian, and the militia commander were also in the carriage, so Sadie was in Merry's lap while Beethoven perched on Gabriel's shoulder. A number of the militia were mounted on horses, riding alongside the carriages.

Time passed slowly; the conversation stilted as they journeyed to the river. A large barge was docked, big enough to hold four carriages at a time, so it took a while before their entire party was on the other side and they could continue their journey. No one suggested splitting up.

With the use of carriages and horses, they traversed through the valley much faster than Merry and her friends had managed alone. It was late afternoon when they made their way closer to the dam. Merry's nerves jangled, expecting an attack at any moment, then flinching when a cry came.

This was it. Time to fight.

Only, when she got out of the carriage, she saw that it was not Karl and his forces they faced.

Water was seeping through cracks in the dam wall, a puddle of it forming at the base. It bore a familiar sickening shine.

A groan and the sound of rocks scraping against each other carried over the breeze.

'The dam is going to burst.' Lady Beatrice, panic etched on her face, turned to Gabriel. 'The valley will be flooded with poisoned water. Do any of your mages have Earth magic?'

Gabriel cast a worried glance at the dam. 'Your message said the problem was with Water, so I brought the strongest Water mages I could gather in such a short time. Some of them have a second mastery, but none are with Earth.'

Lady Beatrice's face went pale. 'There is no time for a mundane solution. To fix those cracks, we need an Earth mage as powerful as the one that helped my great grandfather build the dam. The valley will be flooded, the river poisoned, and there isn't time to evacuate the people in the low-lying areas.'

Merry stared at the dam, stretching out her senses as more water spilled through, the cracks widening. She rummaged in her pack and pulled out the heartstone, feeling the thrum of it through her body. Then she gripped her staff, the heartstone pressed against it, and stepped closer to the dam.

'Merry, no.' Ellen grabbed her arm. 'Master Nelson said you risk full magical exhaustion if you don't rest for at least a week.'

Merry gave her a wry smile. 'I know. But if I don't try, more people could die like that family in the pass.'

Lady Beatrice rounded on Merry, hope brimming in her eyes. 'You are an Earth mage?'

'I'm not properly trained, but I'll try.' With the heartstone amplifying her powers, she hoped her rudimentary magical skills would be enough.

'Wait.' Ellen placed a hand on Merry's shoulder and warmth flooded her body. 'I'll shore up your energy as best I can. That should help.' Now she turned to the assembled mages and witches. 'If any of you have healing ability, be ready to support Merry.'

Two people came forward from the local Water witches, and with them at her back, their hands on her shoulders, Merry faced the dam once more, hoping her untrained magic would be enough. With a deep breath, she started by grounding her Earth senses in the valley itself, immersing herself in the feel of the grasses beneath her feet, the rich dirt their roots were embedded in. Then she travelled through the earth to the base of the dam, her consciousness skimming over the stone.

The tainted water made her head reel and she fought the urge to retch as the stench invaded her senses. She forced her nausea down, imagining being walled off from it. She was stone, immobile, resolute.

The mental stench lessened, and she reached out with her senses to explore the first crack, willing the stone to knit together, using the same litany as she had with the twigs and leaves when patching the leaking boat. Only this time she envisioned the stone expanding to fill the gap and then solidifying again. Exultation filled her as the trickle of tainted water stopped. But this was only the first of many cracks. One by one, she coaxed the stone structures to heal themselves, her breath coming faster and sweat beading on her brow before she was even halfway done. She was aware Ellen and the others were still there supporting her, but she ignored them. All of her being was focused on repairing the dam.

The cracks near the top were bigger, and as she set to work on the largest her head began to pound. She swayed, and then felt warmth flood through her body, dimly aware of the two witches with healing abilities lending their strength.

Even with their help, it was all Merry could do to remain standing as she hastily worked on the last few cracks. She dropped her staff and heartstone, falling to her knees when she was done, pleased but exhausted from her handiwork. Lady Beatrice would have to get a real Earth mage to inspect the hasty repair job, but she was confident the dam wall would hold.

Hands gripped Merry's arms and she was gently

pulled to her feet, finding herself looking into Gabriel's concerned eyes. He wrapped his arms around her back to hold her steady. She placed her hands on his hard chest, tempted to close her eyes and lean fully against him. Just until she regained her strength, of course.

He smelled of mint and there was a hint of crispness to the soft breaths he exhaled. Like a fresh wind on a clear day.

Ellen appeared at her side with a cup of water. 'Master Nelson was kind enough to allow me to replenish my herb supplies. This should help.'

Gabriel shifted his arms but did not let go as Merry took the cup from Ellen and sipped at the tingling water. With each sip she took she felt her energy return, until she reluctantly moved away from Gabriel, no longer in need of his support.

He stayed close as Lady Beatrice came to stand before her.

'Merry, my province owes you a great debt. Thank you.' She bowed her head low. Then she moved off to rally her troops for the incursion into the dam.

Gabriel's smile was strained as he gazed at Merry. 'Are you sure you're all right?'

'Feeling better every minute,' said Merry, before finishing off the last of her magically enhanced water and handing the mug to Ellen to pack away.

'You've done enough,' said Gabriel, clasping Merry's hand. 'From here on, we will take care of the magic.' He waved his free hand towards the assembled Water mages and witches. 'Okay?'

Merry gave him a smile. 'Okay.'

Then she eyed Ellen. 'Did you happen to get any more of those herbs to help ward off the stench?'

The healer gave a nod. 'I don't have many masks made up, so those with the strongest Water magic should have them. If your experience is anything to go by, they are the ones who will be worst hit,' she said as she pulled a series of cloths out of her pack and handed them to Gabriel and the Water mages who had accompanied him from the guild.

She gave the last one to Merry, who fastened it tightly around her lower face. When they came face to face with the tainted stone, she was going to need all the help she could get. The stench from when she had fixed the dam had been bad enough.

'The militia will go in first,' said Lady Beatrice. 'We cannot afford to lose any of our Water users.'

Adrian frowned. 'Your militia will be no match for mages. My enforcers do not possess Water magic, but we can protect your people.'

The two of them argued back and forth, until it was finally agreed that the militia and the enforcers would enter together. As Merry grabbed her belongings and clambered back into the carriage, she risked sending her senses into the dam and discovered the caution had not been necessary. There was no spark of life to indicate anyone with or without magical abilities was within. The dam was empty, except for the poisoned stone.

Her stomach churned as the carriage made its way to the ramp that led to the upper wall of the dam. If they couldn't get rid of the taint, she would be stuck in Tirana forever, and there would be nothing to stop Huntingdon's witch hunters from using the portal once the wards wore off in the bookshop back in Belwich. She had already lost days traipsing across Marshland. She couldn't afford to lose more time.

As the shadow of the dam wall enveloped them, setting a shudder racing down her spine, Merry had a feeling she would not be able to keep her promise not to use her magic again.

CHAPTER 13

Merry led the way down numerous stairwells and through the winding labyrinth of rooms that comprised the interior of the dam, glad they carried lanterns so she didn't need to provide light. She still felt shaky after repairing the dam. Her neck was sore from bending it to avoid being clunked on any low hanging pipe, and the nausea in her stomach made her even more uncomfortable. The mask and Ellen's herbal mix helped to stave off some of the stench, but the closer they got to the poison stone the worse it got. The pins and needles washing over her body grew stronger, and she grit her teeth against the unpleasant sensation.

As she rounded the last bend, the glow from the aquamarine cast a sickly light over the room. It was still suspended in water, but the pipes above and below it had been opened. Merry had sealed the cracks in the dam that the lower pipe led to, so the water was not moving. The stone pulsed with tainted magic, and even looking at it made her queasy. Merry turned sideways, averting her gaze from the stone, as Gabriel and the others entered the room.

Lady Beatrice's face was decidedly green. She had declined the use of a mask, despite being a strong Water witch, but now looked to be regretting that decision. The witches clustered around her also looked ill, and despite having masks, Gabriel and the guild mages looked just as sick as Merry felt.

Gabriel, his eyes bleak above the mask, stepped closer to the tank with the stone, a hand outstretched towards the clear glass.

'Don't touch it,' said Merry, as she stepped to his side. She grabbed his arm to make doubly sure he couldn't ignore her warning. 'Kassandra said the mage who created it died while making the other one. We don't know if the taint could affect you through the glass.'

He gave Merry a quick smile, patting her hand where it rested on his bicep. 'I appreciate your concern, but we have to know what we are dealing with to have any hope of destroying it. I promise though, I will not touch it.'

He let go of Merry's hand as he called the other mages over. 'Keep yourselves shielded as you sense out the stone. Do not engage,' he said.

The mages stared at the stone, only to reel back as one, retching in the corner of the room. Merry winced in sympathy, remembering her first encounter with the source of the taint at the rock pool.

Gabriel's jaw was tight, and his bicep tense under Merry's hand, and she saw him swallow rapidly. His grey eyes were reddened as he gazed at her. 'I have never seen anything like it. The stench, the way it seeps into your mind, is truly monstrous.'

He looked to Lady Beatrice. 'You say the water on the other side of the dam is all like this?' He waved a hand at the blue green water in the tank.

'Yes. Any who drank the water died horrible deaths. Those who came into contact with it also died, but more slowly.' Her expression was grim. 'We have been successful so far in keeping it out of Lower Marshland, but it will eventually seep through the ground. Once it reaches the river the entire province will succumb to the taint, and from there it will spread to the rest of Tirana through the waterways above and below ground.'

Gabriel rubbed his chin as he contemplated the stone. Then he slid Merry's hand off his arm and stepped closer to the tank. 'There has to be a way to stop it. Lord Andel would not risk poisoning the entire country. Lady Beatrice, your message to the guild stated that Karl Piermont had said he would remove the taint once you agreed to support Andel in his push for a monarchy. I wonder...'

He reached out a hand, mere inches separating his palm from the tank, and closed his eyes.

For a long moment nothing happened, everyone

silent as they watched Gabriel. Goose bumps rippled over Merry's skin and she knew he was wielding his magic. More, a current spread through her, one that felt like the ebb and flow of water, and she got the sense he was attempting to manipulate the water around the stone.

She was about to reach out with her own senses when Gabriel groaned. The current and the goose bumps vanished as he slumped to the ground, his entire body shuddering. Horror engulfed Merry as the shine from the taint appeared on the fingers of the hand he'd held near the tank.

Ellen moved towards him, but Merry caught her arm and pulled her back. 'Don't touch him. He's been poisoned.'

'But he didn't touch it,' said Ellen.

'I don't know how, but I can see the taint on his hands.' Her throat closed over as the taint spread to his wrist.

'You're right. I can feel it working its way through his arm.' Ellen held a hand on her heartstone, a horrified look on her face. 'It's heading for his organs.'

Merry gripped her own heartstone and engaged her Earth senses. In her mind's eye the poison stone showed up as a pulsating blue green glow. Back in the mine, Gabriel had shone with a clear blue and white light. Now the blue light was tinged with the same colours as the stone, and a thin ribbon of blue green snaked between his infected hand and the tainted aquamarine.

Somehow, the stone was connected to him.

Worse, the poison stone was getting bigger as she focused on it, as was the pins and needles sensation, while the taint was spreading over Gabriel. The blue spark that represented his Water magic dimmed, but not the white of his Air magic. It was almost as if the stone was sucking him dry of his Water magic to increase its potency.

Acting on instinct, Merry raised her staff and brought it down on the ribbon coming from the stone. The severed ribbon twirled in the air above Gabriel and then shot towards one of the Water mages who had her hands pointed at the stone, lips moving in a spell.

'Stop using any Water magic,' Merry called out as she once again swung her staff to stop the ribbon from connecting with the mage.

As soon as the mage switched off her magic, the ribbon retreated back to the stone. But now that Merry was focused on it with her Earth magic, she could see dozens of ribbons swirling in the water, like jellyfish tentacles. She was sure that if anyone attempted to use Water magic, one of those tendrils would try to latch on to them to suck them dry of their magic.

Still gripping her staff, she kneeled beside Gabriel, using her senses to check him over as best she could. There was no longer any visible sign of the taint on his hand, but that didn't mean he was going to be okay. She looked up at Ellen. 'Can you tell if he is still infected, without touching him?'

Ellen held a hand over Gabriel's head. He was moaning softly, face contorted, but his eyes did not open.

'Physically, he appears all right, although weak. I can see no sign that his organs have been affected.' She hesitated, worry brimming in her gaze. 'But I can sense a disharmony in his gland. The one that allows his magical ability. It almost feels as if part of his consciousness is missing.'

Shock ripped through Merry as Beethoven trotted over to Gabriel and sniffed at his head. Then the grey and white cat turned to Merry. *He is weaker in his Water magic than he was before. I cannot sense any change in his Air magic.*

Merry pushed down her fear for Gabriel as she stood and faced the tank. 'It looked as if the stone was pulling his Water magic out of him, until I severed the connection.' She gestured for Ellen to come up beside her. 'Look at the aquamarine with your healing skills and tell me what you see.'

Ellen gasped. 'It's filled with Water magic. You're right, I can sense part of Gabriel's consciousness in there. Trapped.'

Horror threatened to engulf Merry at the thought of any part of Gabriel's consciousness being trapped in the tainted stone. They had to free him. But how?

When she worked with semi-precious gems for her jewellery, she chose each one carefully before she began creating. Many were not suitable due to inherent flaws, while in others the flaw became part of the piece she was making. None of that had prepared her for dealing with a poisoned aquamarine that stole magic and used it to create a virulent taint that killed all who encountered it.

Or had it?

Most stones had flaws. Maybe this one did too. But to find it she would once again have to use her Earth magic and hope Master Nelson's dire prediction of magical exhaustion did not come true.

With a deep breath, she turned to the assembled people behind her. 'No matter what happens, do not touch me. I may be able to stop the stone from accessing my Water magic, but I won't be able to stop the taint from connecting with anyone I come into contact with while I'm working.'

With her warning given, she blocked off her Water magic as best she could, as she had when she'd used a spell to hide her and Ellen from the hunting militia and mages. She did not want to risk getting drained by the stone as Gabriel had been. Then she carefully stretched out her Earth senses, seeking flaws in the stone itself.

She kept her touch distant. Even then, it was like trying to walk through mud that came to her knees. Heat flashed through her, causing sweat to bead on her face as she worked to keep separate from the magic that pulsed inside the stone and yet to connect with the material it was made from. She imagined herself peering at the aquamarine through a magnifying glass, seeking all the imperfections that made it unique.

She was dimly aware of Ellen and the others watching on, and even of Sadie and Beethoven's mental touch in her mind. She could tell they were all worried about what she was attempting to do, but she had no choice. If they couldn't destroy the stone, and release the magic it imprisoned, Gabriel could die.

With another deep breath, she centred herself, pulling away from the stone to focus on the rock that comprised the dam itself. Steadfast and resolute, the rock was a living presence in her mind, and she used it to wall off the rest of her consciousness. All that remained was Earth. The element throbbed through her, and the other distractions faded away.

The aquamarine shone in her mind, pulsing with oily light though the stench was now gone. She was looking into the heart of the stone itself and could see every flaw it possessed. She selected the largest of them and stepped closer to the tank to place a hand on the glass. She could feel the taint seeking to break through the dam wall she had built around the rest of her sense of self, but the rock remained impervious.

Then she worked on the flaw she had selected, pushing Earth magic into it in the opposite of what she had done with the cracks in the dam wall. She worked to force the flaw to widen, to destabilise the stone.

As she worked, her head throbbed and sweat stung her eyes even though they were closed. Her limbs shook, but she would not stop. She could not stop. She had to break the stone in half.

The magic was in the centre, blocked from escaping by the taint even when she had widened the flaw all the way through. The taint flickered as it was exposed to the water, so Merry set to work on the next largest flaw. One way or another she would destroy this stone and save Gabriel.

The more she widened each individual flaw, the more the stress in the stone increased. The water rippled around it and the taint redoubled its efforts to get through Merry's mental rock wall.

Merry could feel her strength fading. She wished she hadn't told the others not to touch her. She could really do with some extra strength from the healers, but if the taint did manage to use her as a conduit to get to Ellen or the others, she would never forgive herself. At least this way, she was the only one at risk.

She gathered the last of her strength, teeth gritted against the pain in her head as she prepared one last strike. She pictured her staff bright with Earth power and mentally hurled it into the centre of the stone as she commanded it to break. But not just to break. In her head she pictured the taint being leached away as the stone released the stolen Water magic it was using to power itself.

A loud crack reverberated through her head a split second before a blast of pain lashed her entire body. A concussive boom came as the stone shattered into thousands of pieces, the force of the blow pushing Merry back even as the tank walls shattered and water flooded into the room.

Merry scrambled backwards, horrified as she was splattered with parts of the stone and the tainted water. Was she poisoned? Had she just doomed everyone in the room? There was no way they could have avoided being splattered with the tainted water.

Head aching, body throbbing, she got to her feet and forced her limbs to hold her upright. Then a hand gripped her arm, steadying her, and warmth flooded her body.

Another hand gripped her around the waist, and she could smell the familiar minty freshness that was Gabriel. She sagged against him as she surveyed the damage she had caused.

Those with healing ability were tending to shrapnel wounds from the shards of stone, but though many bled from small wounds, no one appeared to be badly injured. Not from the stone itself, anyway.

Merry pulled her mask off and sucked in a deep breath before she thought better of it, and then steeled herself for the smell of the tainted water. The air was clear of the stench, and the pins and needles sensation was gone. She took in another lungful of air, revelling in being able to breathe normally for the first time since they had neared the dam.

As strength returned to her limbs, thanks to Ellen's ministrations, she twisted in Gabriel's arms so she could face him. She cupped his cheek with one hand, her gaze roving over his face. His expression was tight, but he showed no sign of being poisoned.

'You're all right,' she said, running her fingers across the stubble on his firm jaw.

'Thanks to you.' He hugged her tightly, shaking his head slightly. 'I can't believe what you did. It shouldn't have worked. That stone was created from Water magic. Destroying it should have released the taint and infected us all. But somehow you stopped that from happening using Earth magic.'

'Glad I didn't ask if what I was planning was going to work then,' she said with a chagrined smile.

His arms tightened around her as he gazed into her eyes. For a moment it was as if no one else existed. Just her and Gabriel, and she moulded herself against his hard chest, feeling the beat of his heart through her palm.

'If you two are quite finished, there is still the matter of my poisoned province.'

Lady Beatrice's wry tone brought a flush to Merry's cheeks and she eased away from Gabriel. It was a moment before he loosened his grip enough for her to step back. She faced the rest of their group, still flushing.

Adrian stepped forward, giving her a hard stare. 'Can you do what you just did with the stone you believe is within the rock pool?'

Glad for once of his brusque nature, Merry cleared her throat. 'I hope so. But from what I sensed when I was there before, that stone has to be at least twice the size of this one, and creating it killed the mage who made it.'

It had taken every ounce of self-control and strength she had to stop this one, and though she felt physically strong, her head was still aching, and she had a similar feeling to when she had magically exhausted herself getting the leaking boat across the river. She doubted she would be able to destroy the next stone on her own. But if she didn't, she would never get her charm and be able to return home, and one half of Marshland would stay poisoned forever. And it would not stop there. As Lady Beatrice had said, it would eventually seep through the ground and poison more land.

With one last sweep of her Earth magic, she delved deep into the earth, travelling in the direction of the rock pool. Her stomach churned at the pockets of tainted water she found inexorably making their way towards the dam.

The stone had to be destroyed.

'I've been thinking about that,' said Gabriel. 'Mages who share an elemental ability can link together to perform stronger magic. But to do so, they need to trust the others enough to establish the link. We are taught to do this at the guild tower, but I fear we will not be enough. We would need all Water users here to help.' He scanned the Water witches in the room, some sporting healing cuts from the destruction of the stone.

Most of them wore dubious expressions as they

stared back at him. Considering the guild had long disparaged witches as being less, Merry was sure their capacity for trust was low. Even if they did manage to link together, it would not be enough.

'You need more than Water to destroy the stone.' She faced Gabriel and held up a hand when he went to speak. 'More than Air. The minute you try to touch the stone its magic will seek to entrap you. The only way I was able to stop it, was to use Earth to create a mental wall around my Water magic so it couldn't access it. It was Earth magic that destroyed the stone. Water magic removed the taint.'

'Merry, you're the only one here strong enough in Earth magic to even attempt what you're suggesting, and you're already exhausted. If you do this, you risk more than magical exhaustion.' Gabriel shook his head. 'We will have to send to the guild for more Earth mages.'

'We don't have time to wait for reinforcements.' With a sigh, she filled him in on what she'd sensed below ground. 'The poisoned water will soon be so far spread no one will be able to stop it, no matter how strong they are.' Even now, it could be too late. She had no idea how far the taint had reached via the sea. But Merry pushed that thought aside.

'Once we have destroyed the stone in the rock pool, the Water element will be able to repair itself and with it the rest of the poisoned water.' She hoped.

'Tomorrow,' he said, his voice firm. 'Neither of us is in a condition to march through the night.' He looked over at Lady Beatrice. 'We should camp here and make for the rock pool in the morning.'

Lady Beatrice looked torn, but her militia commander stepped to her side. 'Marching in the dark, when we have no idea where our foes have gone, is foolhardy. Mage Fairweather's suggestion is sound.'

After a long moment, Lady Beatrice inclined her head. 'I want guards positioned on the wall and every exit. See to it.'

He gave a nod and then strode off, calling out commands as he went.

Within an hour they had a rudimentary camp set up in the large room Karl Piermont's forces had used. Much of their equipment had been left behind but no one suggested using any of it. Instead they remained in one corner of the space. Marshland militia were given the task of guarding the horses and carriages on top of the wall, there being no way to get them inside the dam.

Ellen bustled about, ensuring the water casks were magically enhanced, Adrian at her side, while Merry found a spot to sit with her back against the wall. She still felt shaky and wondered if it was too early to call it a night.

Gabriel was talking to Lady Beatrice and the militia commander over the other side of the room, but as she watched he excused himself and headed to where several militia guards were handing out food. A moment later he was headed her way with two plates.

'I can't promise military rations are particularly

edible,' he said as he sat beside her and handed her a plate, 'but they are filling, and you must eat to recover your strength. What you did today was incredible, but very draining.'

Merry smiled as she thanked him. She was hungry, and for the next few minutes, she worked her way through the filling but bland meal.

'You still intend to return home, once you have all the charms you need for the transportation spell,' Gabriel said once their meal was finished. 'Is there nothing here that would entice you to stay?'

Merry turned, caught by the intense look in his grey gaze. For a long moment, she couldn't speak. She just stared at him. Then she gave a sigh.

'I have to go home.' She told him about the offer to buy her grandmother's bookshop, and her fears *Huntingdon Inc.* were a front for the witch hunters who had led to Gabriel's ancestors fleeing to Tirana in the first place. 'I have to go home and renew the wards to stop them using the portal.'

'If we destroyed the portal, it would stop them from ever coming here,' he said quietly. 'But then you would never be able to return home.'

Before Merry could respond, he was called on by the militia commander. As he got to his feet, he gazed down at Merry. 'Much as I might wish for you to choose to stay in Tirana, I will do everything I can to ensure you are able to get the remaining charms and complete your spell.'

Conflict set her stomach roiling as he walked away. Gabriel was one of the better things about this magical world she had landed in. She would miss him, and the other friends she had made. Maybe, if she were able to complete her transportation spell and renew the wards around the portal, going home wouldn't mean saying goodbye forever.

But first she had to get the Water charm, and that would mean going up against a crazed enforcer.

You have shown immense resourcefulness since arriving in Tirana. No enforcer, crazed or otherwise, will get the better of you. Your grandmother would be proud.

Merry looked to where Sadie sat beside Beethoven, the two cats watching her with unblinking eyes. Tears pricked her eyes, remembering the outpouring of grief that had come through her link with the little black cat. The familiar had been her grandmother's companion for years. She must be a poor substitute.

No, Merry. Never think that. Sadie got up and moved close enough to rub her head against Merry's hand. *To bond with a witch who is strong in both magic and morals is the goal of any familiar. To be able to do so twice in one lifetime is a miracle. I am honoured to be your companion, Merry Meadows.*

Merry gently stroked Sadie's silky ears. *The honour is mine.*

Later, as Merry made herself comfortable on a borrowed bedroll, Sadie snuggled into her side and Ellen to one side of her, she wondered if they were making a mistake. Was Karl somehow hiding in the dam, waiting until most of them were asleep to launch an attack? She hadn't been able to sense anyone lurking but couldn't discount the idea they might be magically hidden from her Earth sight. After all, she had used magic on a number of occasions to become practically invisible.

But the night passed without an attack, and after a subdued breakfast they packed up and headed to the top of the dam wall and clambered back aboard the carriages. Tension held Merry rigid as her carriage went first down the ramp and they entered the poisoned side of Marshland and set off for the Water focal point.

They travelled in silence for hours, and Merry was starting to think Karl and the others had left Marshland completely when there was a shout of alarm. The carriage jerked to a stop. They scrambled out, Merry's tension returning tenfold as she surveyed the valley before them.

The ground was churned up, with pools of shimmering blue green water collected in shallow craters. Between the craters, uprooted trees sprawled like crayons cast aside by a toddler throwing a tantrum.

'We can't take the carriages through there,' said the Marshland militia commander. 'It would take days to clear the trees. Either we walk through, or we go around. Unless the mages are able to take care of it?' He raised an eyebrow as he turned to face Gabriel.

'It would take Earth magic, to fix this, but Merry is

exhausted as it is. For her to clear this,' said Gabriel as he waved a hand, 'it could push her beyond her limits, causing irrevocable damage.'

Lady Beatrice's expression was cool as she surveyed what had been done to her province. 'Then we walk from here.'

'They'll have prepared an ambush, my lady,' said the militia commander.

Her blue eyes blazed. 'I will not be stopped. This is my land they have poisoned. My people they have murdered with their foul taint. This ends today.' She swept past him and began the laborious process of picking a path through the obstacle course that had been prepared for them.

Merry shared a glance with Gabriel and gave a shrug, and then she set off after Lady Beatrice, hoping that when the expected ambush came they would be ready for it.

CHAPTER 14

Merry's nerves twitched from preparing for an ambush that did not come as they picked their way through the maze of trees and craters of poisoned water. Soon they were out of the valley and the way ahead of them was clear. The stench of the taint here was worse than it had been when Merry and Ellen had first come this way, hanging in the air like a miasma of dread. Even with their masks on, the Water mages were affected. While the witches without masks had covered their faces as best they could, the trek towards the rock pool was punctuated with the sound of retching.

Merry kept her breathing as shallow as she could, not that it helped. The stench overpowered every other scent. Her eyes streamed from the sting of it and bile was a constant presence in the back of her throat. Surely there had to be a better way to ward off the stench. The smell would only get worse the closer they came to the rock pool unless they could come up with some way to clear the air around them.

Air.

She turned to Gabriel, voice nasal as she asked, 'Can you create a wall of air around us, to push back the stench?'

He still appeared weaker than normal, but he gave a nod. 'I'll try.'

Goose bumps swept over her skin as wind whipped round them, creating a vortex that spun around their entire party, pulling the air from near them and funnelling it up into the sky. Merry cautiously took a deeper breath. The stench was still present but not as strong as before.

'How long can you keep that up?' Merry asked.

The skin around Gabriel's eyes tightened. 'As long as I have to.'

While his determination would not falter, she feared his strength would fade long before they reached the rock pool. 'Let it go for now. Conserve your strength for when we really need it.'

She had barely finished speaking when a gout of flame appeared in the sky, aiming straight for them. The stench returned in full as Gabriel used his vortex to spin the flames away.

Shouts came from behind Merry, accompanied by cries of pain and the clashing of swords. She spun around and saw one of the enforcers and a Water mage who had accompanied them to the dam fighting Lady Beatrice's militia.

More traitors!

As Adrian battled against his former colleague with the aid of the remaining enforcers and Marshland militia, two of the Water mages huddled down, clutching their heads. Their fearful moans reminded Merry of when Donna Syphera had used her Spirit magic to insert waking nightmares in the minds of the guards at the gaol back in Greystone.

This had to be the work of Karl's Spirit mage.

Merry left the Fire mage for Gabriel to deal with as she sought out the Spirit mage. She could sense the purple glow his magic emitted, along with a large group of people standing between her party and the rock pool. Karl and Kassandra were among them. She could tell from the red light that showed up on her Earth senses. The two former enforcers hung back as Lord Andel's militia and the mages and witches who had accompanied Karl ran straight towards them and battle ensured. There was sword fighting with the militia and magic fights between the different mages. It was utter chaos. Screams filled the air and the ground beneath Merry's feet undulated.

The local witches under Lady Beatrice's command joined in, doing what they could to aid Adrian and the militia, those like Ellen putting a number of the enemy to sleep with their healing skills. With only poisoned water to call on, the Water witches were hampered, but as the air grew dry Merry knew they were doing every-thing they could.

Merry had her sights set on the Spirit mage, but she hesitated to act. Last time she had faced one she had killed him by opening up a chasm beneath his feet and entombing him within the ground. She did not want to risk that happening again. But, like Gabriel, she could also use Air magic.

The Spirit mage stood beside the Earth mage, and as an ominous crack came from the ground, she knew she had to act. Now.

She flung a funnel of wind at both mages, urging it to twist and turn around them. Their robes flapped furi-ously in the gusts of wind she created. As the mini tornado lifted them into the air, their concentration broke and the attack on the two Water mages stopped, and so did the rumbling in the earth. The Earth mage was shrieking, hands covering her face as the wind spun her about. The Spirit mage quickly regained his compo-sure despite being suspended in the air in the middle of a mini tornado and focused his attention on Merry.

She was ready for him, wrapping a mental rock wall around her consciousness. She could feel him hammering away, trying to break through, but his efforts were puny compared with what the tainted aqua-marine had thrown at her.

She focused on the wind, forming two swirling whips. With a wince, she flung the whips around the mages, tightening them, cutting off their air. The Earth mage went limp, while the Spirit mage was reeling in mid-air, clearly dazed, his mental attack fading away. She lowered them both to the ground and released the wind she'd called, keeping a careful watch as one of Adrian's enforcers rushed over. Was she a traitor?

No. The enforcer formed two fists and both mages' bodies stiffened. Immobilised.

Merry turned back to the main battle, jaw dropping at the sight of Gabriel using Air to defend the Water witches huddled behind Lady Beatrice. He was magnificent. Feet planted firmly, robe whipping around him, arms spread wide, determination etched on his face as he wielded multiple strands of wind to knock projectiles out of the air.

To the left of him, Adrian was standing over Ellen as she worked to heal an injured militia guard, Sadie and Beethoven crouched at her side. The enforcer looked just as determined at Gabriel as he used telekinesis to stop Lord Andel's militia from getting near her. Behind them, the Marshland militia watched over captured foes, with the aid of the remaining three enforcers. Merry was pleased to see the Water mage and the enforcer who had proved to be traitors sprawled unconscious on the ground.

She faced forward again, blinking at the sight of Karl and Kassandra retreating over the hill, the rest of their forces at their backs. Should she pursue them? Stop them from getting away?

Merry shook her head.

No. That was not her fight. She was here to help remove the taint from the rock pool and to get her charm.

'Cowards.' Lady Beatrice appeared at Merry's side; her top lip curled as she watched her enemies retreat. 'I will see to it they pay dearly for what they have done. But first this land must be cleansed.' Now she turned to Merry. 'Are you ready to continue? I will not allow my people to suffer any longer.'

They left all the enforcers save for Adrian and half of the militia from Marshland behind to watch the captured foe. Ellen had rendered all the magic users unconscious, including the Spirit and Earth mages, so they should cause no trouble. The Fire mage had managed to flee with Karl and the others, and it made Merry uneasy to know they were still out there.

Lady Beatrice was right. Cleansing the rock pool was the priority.

As they resumed their trek, and the stench filled every breath Merry took, she feared this battle would not be easily won. The sensation of pins and needles grew stronger than ever before, painfully so.

When they finally arrived at the rock pool, her skin felt like she had been scraped raw by coarse sandpaper and the stench from the tainted stone had tears streaming from Merry's eyes. It was so bad that even those without magic began to experience the effects. She forced her nausea down and set to work on sensing where the stone was hidden.

There it was, in the centre of the rock pool, somehow suspended in the water. It pulsed in her mind's eye, oozing an oily presence as her Earth senses drew closer to it.

Merry groaned and opened her eyes, turning to Gabriel. 'This one is three times the size of the one in the dam. I doubt any shield of Air would be strong enough to protect us from the backlash when it explodes. Even both of us together may have trouble controlling it, let alone being able to wield Water magic to remove the taint.'

He clenched his jaw, determination glinting in his eyes. 'If we link with the others, it should magnify all of our abilities and give us the added strength we need, like twining many smaller strands of rope together to make a far stronger one.'

'Should?'

'Nothing like this has been attempted before. Normally a link is meant for a specific purpose, comprising one flow of magic for whoever controls the link to wield. It's not meant to be spilled into multiple elemental flows, which is what this will entail.'

'So how do you want to work this link?' She envisioned all of them holding hands while Gabriel wielded the combined magic of all the mages and witches present. Or would it be like when Ellen and the others had lent her their strength when she had repaired the cracks in the dam?

Gabriel fixed his gaze on Merry, conviction brimming in his grey eyes. 'I want you to take the lead.'

'Me?' Merry took a step back. 'I have no training. I act on instinct and my magic has a tendency to do whatever it wants.'

'That's why it should be you. Your lack of training means you are unencumbered with the restrictions that come from years of being told there is a certain way to perform magic. You have already cast spells I would have thought impossible, because you let your instincts guide you. Besides, I have mastery of Air and Water only. You used Earth magic to destroy the first stone. If I were to control the link, it would not respond to me. You have to be the one to do it.'

Merry considered him. Was it true? Did her lack of training give her an advantage? Would her instinct be enough to guide her?

She gave a sigh. 'What do I have to do?'

'To participate in a link, mages have to lower their mental defences and allow the person in charge of the link to access their abilities. In doing so, the minds become entwined for the duration of the link. What one thinks, they all think. It allows the wielder of the link to use the combined magic without hesitation.' He visibly hesitated before adding, 'In the past, unscrupulous mages used it to control those of lesser ability to make them perform acts they would not otherwise do and to embed commands that they would follow even when the link was terminated. Therefore, it involves a level of trust and intimacy that has seen the practice fall away.'

Merry scanned the people arrayed around them, hanging back and waiting for their orders. To link with them would be to open herself up. To be in control. They were strangers, and she did not want to have to link with their minds, let alone control them in any way. From the dubious expressions on some of their faces, they were just as reluctant.

She faced Gabriel again. 'Are you sure a link is the only way? What if we all just focus on doing the same thing at the same time?'

'No matter how focused we would try to be, individuals' minds work in different ways. To be truly unified, to have a level of power necessary for what we need to do, it must be wielded by one mage. You.'

He must have seen her reluctance, for he added, 'But there is a way for us to alleviate the need for you to link with all those here. If they link with me first, and then I link to you, you will only be connected to me. But the chain will still work.'

Merry stared at him. Linking with Gabriel would entwine their minds. She gazed into his sincere grey eyes. He had arrested her when they first met, but since they had worked together to stop Lord Andel mining heartstones he had acted in good faith. He had promised not to try to arrest her or make her go to the guild tower against her will, and even before then he had saved her life back at Breezeway after she had dispelled the wind golem. She remembered the way he had cradled her to his chest afterwards, and the other times he had held her, and the reluctance he evidenced when it came time to let go.

She had enjoyed being in his arms, and even thinking about it stirred her senses. But did she trust him enough to link her mind to his?

Merry took a deep breath and gave a nod. 'Okay then, let's do this.'

Gabriel called all those with Water and Earth magic over, including Lady Beatrice, Master Nelson and Ellen. 'What we are attempting to do will be extremely dangerous. If Merry fails, those of us who are linked to her will also succumb. If you are not ready and willing to give your life to rid Marshland of this taint, then you need to say so now. Otherwise, be prepared to link your mind to mine so that Merry will have access to all the power we possess to help her destroy the poison stone.'

Lady Beatrice was the first to step forward, head high and a proud expression on her face. 'As hereditary ruler of Marshland, it is my duty and honour to fight for my land and my people. If that should lead to my death, then so be it. I am prepared.'

After her statement, all the magic users from her province stepped forward and asserted their willingness to link with Gabriel. Then it was the guild Water mages. They faced Gabriel with stern expressions, and for a moment Merry was sure they were going to refuse. Then they stepped forward.

The mage Merry had stopped from being connected to the poison stone in the dam sent a proud look her way as she said, 'We have vowed to uphold guild law, and protect the citizens of Tirana from magic that is ill-used, and against the advent of tyranny. We are duty bound to do everything we can to destroy the poison stone. But even if we were not bound by our vows, we would be honoured to aid Miss Meadows to rid Marshland Province of this taint and to therefore protect all of Tirana.'

Ellen lifted her chin and eyed Merry. 'I have supported you all the way. I'm not stopping now.'

Merry's stomach plummeted at the thought of the link failing and taking Ellen down with her. Bad enough that Gabriel and the others could be lost.

She was stopped from protesting her friend's involvement when Gabriel shook his head. 'We need you to remain clear of the link, Miss Hayland. Your healing skills, along with those of Master Nelson's, are too valuable to risk. I need you to be ready to heal any of us that falter.'

For a long moment, Merry thought Ellen would still insist on being part of the link. But then Adrian stepped to her side and said, 'It is the duty and burden of a healer to heal. Not to fight.'

The young healer gave a sigh. 'Very well, I will remain clear of the link.'

'Thank you,' said Gabriel, bowing his head. Then he faced Adrian. 'We will be vulnerable while we are linked to Merry and focused on destroying the stone and ensuring its taint is cleansed. We trounced Piermont's forces before, but that doesn't mean he won't try again.'

The brusque enforcer captain gave a sharp nod. 'I will watch your back, Mage Fairweather.'

Ellen turned to Merry. 'Be careful. You may be wielding magic that comes from others, but there will still be a toll on you. If at any time you feel at risk of magical exhaustion, you need to sever the link. Promise me you'll be careful.'

Merry gave a nod, throat choking up at the barely concealed worry on her friend's face. They hugged briefly, with Merry reluctant to let go until a sharp sting at her ankle drew her attention to Sadie.

The black cat stood side by side with Beethoven, her yellow eyes gleaming. *See that you follow the healer's advice. I cannot return to Belwich without you, and I will not stand for spending the rest of my life in a world that does not have electricity.*

Merry formed a shaky smile at the tart tone of the familiar's voice, sensing the love and concern that prompted the words. As with Ellen, she had no words, and settled for one final stoke of Sadie's silky soft ears.

Then she turned to Gabriel. 'I'm ready.'

Gabriel ushered those who were to link with him closer, getting them to sit cross legged on the ground before him. Then he led them in a light meditation chant that set waves of goose bumps washing over Merry.

The goose bumps increased in strength, drowning out the pins and needles, and the air shimmered around Gabriel. The feel of magic rolled off him in waves as he turned to face Merry and held out his hands.

If she'd thought she was attracted to him before, seeing him now, brimming with magical energy and ready to share it with her, she was astounded. His eyes shone with an inner light, one that entranced her as she reached out to grasp his hands.

Warmth flooded her body. It wasn't the way it had been when Ellen or Master Nelson had healed her. This was a torrent of heat that swept through her, caressing every part of her being. She could sense Gabriel within the torrent, his emotions coming through, and she got an image in her head. It was an image of her.

Merry was stunned by how beautiful and entrancing she looked. Her light purple hair shone like a halo around her head, framing her face. Her eyes gleamed and her smile was a mix of sultry and sweet, and underscoring it all was a profound sense of admiration.

Was that how he saw her?

How could she ever live up to the perfect image? She was just Merry, bumbling her way through things she did not fully understand.

A wave of reassurance came through from Gabriel, and she got the impression he was seeking to communicate in images if not in words. She saw a series of images, her facing the wind golem, fierce and unafraid. Facing down Lord Andel and Mage Fowler at the mine, and now scared and yet determined as she prepared to face the poison stone in the heart of the rock pool.

Still, even as he gave of himself to show her how he saw her, Merry hesitated to complete the link. He was so sure she would succeed, but what if she didn't? If she failed, she would take him and all the others she could sense linked to him to their deaths.

A rueful smile curving his lips, Gabriel gently tugged her closer and his mouth covered hers. She lost herself in his kiss, the feel of his lips roving over hers, tasting, teasing. The warmth that had flared through her before became an inferno as she deepened the kiss. She melted against his chest, her hands grasping him as she sought to get as close as physically possible. Thoughts of the stone, the magic users linked with Gabriel, and what she was supposed to be doing vanished.

All that existed was him.

There was a stretching inside her head, and her world expanded to wrap around him, and she gasped as a rush of power swept through Gabriel's body and into hers.

She had never felt more alive, more connected with the world around her. She could feel everything. The rustle of the wind against the grass, the minuscule movements of bugs in the earth and the beating hearts of the people who were connected to her, and those that weren't. She could feel Ellen's concern for her wellbeing, Adrian's brusque exasperation that the link was taking too long. In a dim corner she felt Lady Beatrice's pain at the depth of Gabriel's feelings for another woman.

With a gasp, Merry broke off the kiss to stare in stunned silence at Gabriel. His eyes were heavy lidded as he gazed at her, his arms tight around her. With an air of reluctance, he moved back, though he maintained a hold of one hand as Ellen handed Merry her heartstone and staff. Then together, they faced the rock pool.

With the rush of magical energy filling her veins, it was easy for Merry to delve her consciousness through blue green tinged water to the poisoned stone. It was suspended in the water with no apparent form of support, and unlike the one in the dam there was a sense of repulsion, as if it was trying to push her mental probe away.

She deftly avoided the probe and focused on the flaws within the stone, as she had in the dam. But this time she didn't intend on making the stone explode. Instead she worked to gently coax the flaws to spread and allow the magic stored inside it to be released gradually.

As she worked, she got the sense of another presence, an unfamiliar mind not part of her link with Gabriel. An image appeared, showing a man, with grey receding hair and a weak chin, kneeling beside the rock pool as the stone formed in the air in front of him. This was the mage who had created the stone. The image played out, showing him at first in control of the magic he poured into the stone, and then he stiffened, pain wreathing his features as the magic poured out in a rush. Then panic bloomed as he sought to break off the stream. Merry could do nothing but watch as the stone drained the mage completely, leaving his body bereft of all magic and crumpled on the edge of the rock pool.

Was this a memory?

A new vision started, one showing Merry and all the people linked with her having their magic drained, and she realised it was a warning. The stone must have a level of sentience and it was trying to persuade her to stop what she was doing.

But she would not stop, even when the vision vanished, and a cold sense of determination emanated from the stone as it sought to burrow though her mental barrier to reach the kernel of her Water magic. Sweat beaded Merry's brow as she reinforced the stone wall around her mind, drawing on more power through the link to do so. If the wall fell, the stone would be able to access the minds of Gabriel and the others and drain them too. She could not let that happen.

She straightened her back, murmuring a litany under her breath to keep the mental wall impervious, even as she worked with her Earth magic to spread the flaws in the stone wider.

Little by little, wisps of magic escaped the stone and Merry could feel it getting weaker. Smaller. It was working. She just had to keep up her fault enhancement.

But even as the stone shrank further, Merry sensed a lessening in the strength she had access to. In the dark reaches of her mind she realised that some of the weaker witches had passed out, no longer able to sustain the link. One by one they fell, and the strain on Merry's own power grew. Soon there was only the guild mages and Gabriel left in the link, the weight of those rendered unconscious drawing them down.

With one last lurch, the mages fell away and it was only her and Gabriel left.

Merry could sense a rising in the stone as it prepared to batter her mental wall and she stopped working on the faults to protect her connection with Gabriel. She would not let the stone hurt him.

With a massive effort she broke off the link with Gabriel, releasing his hand, and faced the stone on her own. With both hands now clasped around her heartstone and staff, she commanded it to yield, drawing it towards her. It rose out of the rock pool, now smaller than her fist, spinning in the air.

It hung above the centre of the rock pool. Merry could see it clearly both with her physical vision and her mind's eye and threw everything she had into squeezing out every last drop of stolen magic. She could feel her body trembling, and shouts coming from Ellen and the others, but she ignored them. The stone would not win.

She dropped her mental wall and threw every ounce of Water magic she had at it and a blast of pure blue speared into the centre of the aquamarine. It flashed so brightly she had to close her eyes. Even then she could still see it.

As weariness swamped her, she saw the stone, now as small as her thumbnail, floating towards her. No hint of the taint remained though it pulsed with an inner light. The light spread to encompass the rock pool and destroyed the taint that smothered the water within.

Merry reached out a hand and plucked the aquamarine out of the air. The moment she touched it, a sense of connection, similar to what she felt with her heartstone, thrummed through her and she realised it was her new charm. In the distance she was aware of the blue light she had unleashed spreading though the underground water tunnels as well as ascending the waterfall to the river above, clearing away the taint as it went.

She tried to turn to face Gabriel and the others, but her body didn't respond. The pulsing of the stone washed over her and the last thing she heard was Sadie's despairing cry echoing through her head as the world went dark.

CHAPTER 15

*M*erry blinked, finding it hard to open her eyes. Her thoughts were muffled, as though they were stuffed in cotton wool. She shifted position in the bed, the mattress beneath her enfolding her softly.

Bed?

The last thing she remembered was plucking her new charm out of the air before passing out beside the rock pool.

As she struggled to a sitting position some of the fog left her head, though there was still a muffling effect. She leaned back against a timber headboard and looked at the plush coverlet covering her lower body. It was purple velvet shot through with silver threads.

Was she back at Lady Beatrice's manor? If she was, this was not the room she had shared with Ellen. The bed was much larger, the linen softer and made of a finer weave. She scanned the room and saw a fireplace directly across from the bed. But that was not what caught her attention.

Her gaze was riveted on the young man in a blue and white robe, his long legs stretched out in front of him as he slept in a wing backed chair to the left of the fireplace.

Gabriel.

Merry tossed the bedding aside and slid out of bed, her bare feet sinking into a plush carpet. She was wearing a flowing white nightgown with long sleeves, that covered her from neck to toe. As she walked across the room to where Gabriel slept, her feet made no sound. She scanned the rest of the room and saw two doors, one closed and the other open to reveal a bathroom. A large wooden cupboard was nested within an alcove set in one wall.

There were no windows, the fire offering the only light as she reached Gabriel's side and stared down at him, remembering the encompassing nature of the kiss they had shared at the rock pool. That kiss had allowed her to link with him so thoroughly they had been as one.

His dark lashes brushed his cheeks. As she watched, his eyes fluttered open and he shifted position. His clear grey gaze locked onto her.

'Morning,' said Merry, smiling at him. 'Well, I guess it's morning. There's no window, so I can't tell what time it is.'

He did not smile back. If anything, his expression

darkened as he straightened up, wiping at his face. She saw him swallow heavily before he stood.

'Sit, please,' he said, waving at the chair he had just occupied. 'There is something I need to tell you.'

Merry frowned. Even when he had been trying to arrest her, he had never been so grave. 'Why do I think it's not good news.' She sucked in a breath. 'Did it not work?' She'd been sure she had sensed the blue light, pure Water magic, removing the taint from the water before she passed out. But maybe it hadn't been enough?

'It worked,' he said as he moved to light a lantern set on the mantle above the fireplace. The room brightened though his expression did not as he turned back to face her. 'You saved Marshland Province, and for that you should be celebrated as a hero. Not locked up in here.' He waved his hand at the room.

'Locked up?' Merry hadn't taken his advice to sit and now surged across the room to the closed door. She twisted the handle, but it did not move.

She spun back to face Gabriel.

'I'm sorry,' he said, shaking his head. 'I had no choice. It was the only way to save you.'

The implications of his words sank in. 'I'm in the guild tower.'

Her legs threatened to buckle under her. He rushed to her side and tried to wrap an arm around her, but she warded him off as she staggered over to the chair he had been sleeping in and sat heavily.

He kneeled in front of her, reaching for her hand.

'You magically exhausted yourself in defeating the stone. You lapsed into a coma and there was nothing Ellen and Master Nelson could do to wake you up. You were fading, your body wasting away. I had to bring you here, to the guild healers, to save your life.' His breath hitched as he said, 'If not for Ellen keeping you going, you would not have survived the journey.'

'Alive. But as a guild prisoner.' She pulled her hand free from his grasp. 'I'm not going to be allowed to leave to get the last two charms, and go home to my world, am I?'

He shook his head. 'I tried to convince my aunt that you should be set free, but she would not listen. Though you were not born in Tirana, she has decreed that your bloodline makes you subject to guild laws. As such, you will be required to swear an oath to obey those laws and trained to master your abilities here at the tower. Once she is assured of your loyalty to the guild, you will be permitted to leave.'

Leave the tower. But not Tirana. She would be stuck here for the rest of her life, either locked up in this room or as a guild mage.

She shook her head, jaw tensing. 'I am not staying here. I have to get home. Those witch hunters could be working on a way to get through the portal as we speak. Did you tell her that? That I have to go home and reinforce the wards around my grandmother's bookshop?'

'My aunt does not believe the hunters will be able to open the portal. They would need a powerful spell to unlock it, and no one exists on the other side to make one for them. She feels that if you were to continue to make your transportation spell, you would be the one to put Tirana at risk by returning to your world with it, allowing it to fall into the hands of the witch hunters.'

Merry stilled. Would returning with a transportation spell endanger Tirana?

No. Her grandmother had been protecting the portal for years and no witch hunters had gained access. Merry could do the same. Besides, with the way things were developing in Tirana, the guild would not remain in power much longer. Revolution was coming, and Merry did not want to be caught up in it. She was getting out of there.

She got up and strode over to the door again, reaching for her Earth magic to crush the lock.

But there was nothing there. Just that muffled sense she'd had since waking.

She tried again, focusing on the stone wall around the door. She would tear it loose and use her Air magic to push aside anyone who got in her way.

Again, there was no response from her magic.

'Break!' Anger thrummed through her as she commanded the wooden door to destroy itself.

'Your magic won't work in here,' said Gabriel, coming up to stand beside her. He had a hand up, as if he wanted to touch her, but she whirled away from him and shook her head.

No. This was not happening.

Sadie, can you hear me? She put everything she had into the mental call to her grandmother's familiar, heart pounding as she waited for a response.

Nothing. Just the empty echo of her words in her head.

With a despairing cry, Merry grabbed hold of the door handle and wrenched at it again and again, her movements frenzied. But the handle did not move. The door did not open. She was trapped.

She sagged against the door.

Trapped in the guild tower with no way out.

Unless…

'You can get me out of here.' She spun and faced Gabriel. 'You brought me here, even though you promised me you wouldn't do that against my will.'

He shook his head. 'I wish I could, but you are not the only prisoner here. My aunt no longer trusts me. I was allowed to be here, for when you woke up, but soon the enforcers will come to escort me back to my own gilded prison.' He waved a hand to the door. 'This entire floor of the tower is warded against elemental magic. Only enforcer magic works here, and the ones guarding us are unquestionably loyal to the guild and my aunt. She has demanded I also swear the oath to obey. I am to remain here until I agree to do so.'

Merry stared in horror at him. 'What are we going to do?'

Gabriel moved forward to wrap his arms around her.

'We prove our loyalty to the guild by taking the oath. It is the only way to be free of this place.'

To swear an oath was to forswear her freedom. There was no way she was doing that.

Her grandmother had found a way out of this warded tower. Merry would, too.

No way was she swearing an oath to the guild that had ruined so many lives.

A knock came at the door and moments later two enforcers entered. She pushed away from Gabriel, ignoring the entreaty in his eyes as the enforcers led him away.

She moved over to the fireplace and sank into the chair, staring into the flames. She had never felt more lost since arriving in Tirana. She was on her own, imprisoned in a tower above one of the focal points she needed to access to get her next charm. The focal point may as well have been on the other side of Tirana for all the good it did her.

She would bide her time. No matter what, she would escape and finish the spell she needed to get home.

Somewhere out there, Lord Andel, Karl Piermont and all their allies were plotting to bring the guild down. They would force all magic users to swear an oath to obey the new king, including Ellen and the other friends she had made. They were all in danger, and the only thing Ophelia Fairweather cared about was the guild and maybe getting revenge on Merry's dead grandmother.

All this on account of a woman she had never known existed until a couple of weeks ago.

Merry got up and began to inspect every inch of the room she was trapped in. The open door led to a sumptuous bathroom filled with all manner of soaps and with indoor plumbing that was modern by Tiranian standards. With a wry twist to her mouth, she wondered if all guild prisoners were kept in such luxurious confines. In the timber wardrobe were a number of simple dresses in green, blue and white, the elements she had displayed an ability for. In the bottom was a bag containing her grandmother's spell box, the charms she had so far collected still jumbled inside with the broken spell that had brought her to Tirana.

Merry picked up the heartstone, striving to find the connection she had felt with it. But it was simply a pretty stone now, as was the aquamarine she had almost died to collect. She picked it up and weighed it in her palm. If not for this stone, she would never have magically exhausted herself and required guild healing. Although, if Ophelia Fairweather didn't have such a stranglehold on mages Merry's friends might have been able to find a closer healer with mage strength. She might as well wish that Lord Andel and Karl had never come up with the idea to poison the water in Marshland or that she had signed the contract to sell *Merry Magic* the moment the solicitor had given it to her.

With a sigh, she placed the aquamarine back in the box and ran her fingers over the feather from the legendary silver falcon. No matter what her current predicament, she would not wish away the experiences and the friends she had made since arriving in Tirana. Even Gabriel. As conflicted as he was by his loyalty to his aunt, he had tried to do the right thing and been locked up in a room across the corridor. He was as much a victim in this as she was, and she wished she hadn't been so abrupt with him before he'd been escorted out.

She closed the spell box and placed it back in her bag, her fingers brushing against the familiar wood of her staff. She tugged on it, musing that she could at least use it to hit someone with if not to focus her magic.

One end of the staff caught on something in the back of the wardrobe and Merry pushed aside the dresses to see what it was snagged on. A thin leather strap was caught on the end and she tugged it free, and then pulled on the strap.

Her eyes widened as the back of the wardrobe moved and a glint of pure light gleamed through a small gap no bigger than her spell box. Merry thrust her hand into the gap, searching for the source of the light. She pulled out an amethyst and a small notebook with a plain leather cover. The light emitted by the amethyst died as soon as she removed it from the gap.

She put it back and the light shone once more.

Merry smiled as she realised what was happening. The amethyst was magic, and warded though the tower might be, here was a place where it still worked. She replaced the cover over the gap and closed the wardrobe before going to the chair by the fire to inspect the book.

She opened the cover and stared at the words neatly penned in handwriting she had seen only once before, in the letter from her grandmother.

This book had belonged to Meredith Meadows, and as Merry flicked through the cream pages she was sure that it would contain everything she needed to know to escape the guild.

ACKNOWLEDGMENTS

As always, writing the book is only part of the process.

I would like to thank Sally Odgers for her editing skills and her eagerness to continue to read and fine tune my stories. Sue-Ellen, Danni, Donna and Jennifer have my sincere thanks for beta reading, typo hunting, and helping to make sure the final version is the best it can be.

Pixie Covers has once again created a stunning cover that catches the eye and embodies the spirit of *Merry Magic*. Merry would not exist if not for the original set of Pixie Covers that inspired her story.

It has been a year of ups and downs, and my family has been there every step of the way to cheer me on and they don't complain too much when I hide away in my writing cave. While the furbabies are good at making me take a break by insisting on cuddle time.

Finally, to the readers who have taken a chance on

Merry and are following along on her adventures, thank you thank you thank you. It means so much to me to know that readers love Merry and her story as much as I do. You are a huge part of why I keep writing.

Here's to always being able to create magic with words.

ABOUT THE AUTHOR

Shelley Russell Nolan is an avid reader who began writing her own stories at sixteen. Her first completed manuscript featured brain eating aliens and a butt kicking teenage heroine. Since then she has spent her time creating fantasy worlds where death is only the beginning and even freaks can fall in love.

The first two books in her debut adult urban fantasy series, *Lost Reaper* and *Winged Reaper*, were published by Atlas Productions in 2016, with *Silver Reaper* published in 2017 to complete the series. 2018 saw the release of her *Arcane Awakenings Novella Series*, while Odyssey Books published the first book in a new post-apocalyptic series in 2019.

Born in New Zealand, moving to Australia with her family when she was seven, Shelley currently lives in Central Queensland, Australia, with her husband and two young children. They share their home with two wrecking ball kitties, and two crazy dogs.

Shelley loves to hear from her readers so feel free to contact her on Facebook or leave a review where you purchased this book, on Goodreads or on her website - shelleyrussellnolan.com

9 780648 168393